CALEB'S HEALING STORY

by the same author

A Safe Place for Caleb
An Interactive Book for Kids, Teens and Adults with Issues
of Attachment, Grief, Loss or Early Trauma
Kathleen A. Chara and Paul J. Chara, Jr.
Illustrated by J.M. Berns
ISBN 978 1 84310 799 6
eISBN 978 1 84642 143 3

Amy Elizabeth Goes to Play Therapy
A Book to Assist Psychotherapists in Helping Young Children
Understand and Benefit from Play Therapy
Kathleen A. Chara and Paul J. Chara, Jr.
Illustrated by J.M. Berns
ISBN 978 1 84310 775 0

Sensory Smarts
A Book for Kids with ADHD or Autism Spectrum Disorders
Struggling with Sensory Integration Problems
Kathleen A. Chara and Paul J. Chara, Jr. with Christian P. Chara
Illustrated by J.M. Berns
ISBN 978 1 84310 783 5

Allergy Busters
A Story for Children with Autism or Related Spectrum
Disorders Struggling with Allergies
Kathleen A. Chara and Paul J. Chara, Jr. with Karston J. Chara
Illustrated by J.M. Berns
ISBN 978 1 84310 782 8

CALEB'S
HEALING STORY

**AN INTERACTIVE STORY WITH ACTIVITIES TO HELP
CHILDREN TO OVERCOME CHALLENGES ARISING FROM
TRAUMA, ATTACHMENT ISSUES, ADOPTION OR FOSTERING**

KATHLEEN A. CHARA AND TASHA A. LEHNER

ILLUSTRATED BY SAMANTHA ABURIME

Jessica Kingsley *Publishers*
London and Philadelphia

First published in 2016
by Jessica Kingsley Publishers
73 Collier Street
London N1 9BH, UK
and
400 Market Street, Suite 400
Philadelphia, PA 19106, USA

www.jkp.com

Library of Congress Cataloging in Publication Data
A CIP catalog record for this book is available from The Library of Congress

British Library Cataloguing in Publication Data
A CIP catalogue record for this book is available from the British Library

ISBN 978 1 78592 702 7
eISBN 978 1 78450 245 4

Printed and bound in Great Britain

Contents

Acknowledgment

We thank Bruce Buchanan for his permission to present some of his techniques for working with attachment problems.

Introduction for Parents, Caregivers, and Professionals

The secret of getting ahead is getting started.

—Mark Twain

Caleb's Healing Story is the second book written from the perspective of young Caleb Smith about healing from his attachment issues and early trauma. In the first book, *A Safe Place for Caleb*, theories and definitions as well as therapeutic interventions regarding attachment, trauma, grief, and loss are explored (Chara and Chara 2005). *A Safe Place for Caleb* outlines five main goals for resolving trauma that can lead to disrupted attachment as well as grief and loss issues:

1. Resolve past trauma / losses.

2. Reconstruct cognitive beliefs based on these experiences.

3. Assist with the development of trust.

4. Learn to handle emotions appropriately.

5. Understand societal expectations and learn to engage in reciprocal relationships within a safe and family-focused environment.

In *Caleb's Healing Story*, readers are invited to join Caleb on a healing journey by sharing their own stories and completing the healing activities included in Part 2 of the book. *Caleb's Healing Story* expands the goals for resolving trauma by identifying specific common challenges that children / teens with a history of attachment problems and trauma encounter on a daily basis and offers easy-to-use interventions in the form of activities and worksheets. The identified common challenges and the interventions presented are compiled based on both Kathleen and Tasha's clinical counseling experience working with many children and their families.

HOW TO USE THIS BOOK

The first half of this book is a story designed for the person struggling with attachment and trauma issues. The story is written from the perspective of Caleb, a composite figure based on experiences with several clients that Kathleen had the privilege to walk with during their healing journeys. Reading about Caleb's experience facilitates an understanding of common challenges and offers hope for healing. Many children/teens find Caleb's story of experiencing abuse and neglect, having difficulty trusting others, and being adopted easy to relate to. Readers join Caleb on their own healing journey by answering questions, drawing pictures, reading motivational quotes, learning positive affirmations, and completing healing activities related to each chapter.

We have found that many behavioral issues displayed by children/teens with trauma and attachment issues are really fear-based. Therefore, the activities and worksheets are designed based on our clinical experiences to help readers recognize and change these fear-based thoughts and behaviors. (You may want to make additional copies of the worksheets so they can be used more than once by each child/teen.) We also acknowledge that it can be especially challenging for parents and caregivers to understand that even when a child/teen is displaying rage or disrespect, these behaviors are often rooted in fear caused by trauma. When a child/teen is acting out of fear, it is helpful to tell yourself things like, "That was her hurt talking" or "That was his trauma talking." As a result, we have included additional activities to support parents and caregivers with their struggles in caring for a child/teen who has experienced trauma and/or attachment breaks. We encourage parents and caregivers to listen closely to how the struggles Caleb shares in the story exist throughout his entire day, not just at certain times. Trauma is not something that can just be turned off—it takes hard work to achieve healing.

In addition to activities and worksheets, we have also included assessment measures that we designed to be completed by both parents/caregivers and the reader (with or without the help of mental health professionals). The purpose of these assessments is to identify areas of concern and to have an appropriate means to measure improvements. At the end of reading each chapter, you will be prompted to complete related assessments and activities. We recommend completing the assessment Common Challenges for Children and Teens (page 74) first and using this as a guideline for choosing additional assessments and activities to complete.

USE BY PROFESSIONALS IN A THERAPEUTIC SETTING

This book can be used as a stand-alone book for professionals as well as a companion to *A Safe Place for Caleb*. We encourage mental health professionals to consider using both books not only for individual and family counseling, but also for conducting a variety of group counseling formats. We have included additional guidelines and recommendations for using this book in a therapeutic setting (see Guidelines and Recommendations for Professionals, page 133). Teachers in a classroom setting can also use this book.

USE IN A FAMILY OR NON-THERAPEUTIC SETTING

We designed this book to be read together by a child/teen and a trusted adult. While the story is being read, adults should explain new concepts, such as *Early Hurts* and the *Hurt Self* (a glossary of terms is presented in the back of the book). Some kids may want to read Caleb's entire story all the way through first and then go back to do the activities and questions on the second read-through. We want to stress that the activities we designed for this book are not to be done by the child/teen alone. Rather, children and teens with attachment and trauma issues are to work with a parent or adult who is motivated to assist in their healing. It is important to understand that healing from *Relational Injury* requires a healthy relationship with another person as part of the healing process. Sometimes parents question if their teen will benefit from a book with a main character who may appear much younger than the teen. However, if your teen had *Relational Injury* much earlier in his or her life, this book takes readers back to those early experiences that still need healing.

When reading the book and completing the activities and assessments, it is recommended that you read about a chapter a week with your child/teen. Keep in mind, it is very important to go at the pace of the child/teen. Spend more time on chapters and activities that highlight the Common Challenges that your child/teen identifies as most difficult. After completing the activities related to each chapter, celebrate your child/teen's achievements and healing journey! Even if the progress may seem small, it takes hard work and is worth celebrating.

Remember: "A journey of a thousand miles starts with a single step"— Lao Tzu.

We applaud you and your family as you continue on your journey towards healing. As Caleb once said, "Push past the pain. You deserve to be loved and to love the ones who love you." We are both passionate about helping families to heal, and we wish you all the very best as you take this healing journey together.

Here's to Healing Kids all over the world,

Kathleen

Kathleen

Tasha

Tasha

PART 1

CALEB'S STORY

CALEB'S STORY

Characters

(In order of appearance)

Caleb—That's me!

CHARACTERS FROM MY ADULT LIFE

Rosa—My wife. She is a great mom to our children. She likes to paint.

Billy—My son. He is five years old and loves to play with trains.

Felicia—My daughter. She reminds me of my baby sister Kelly because of her silly laugh and her love for her big brother.

CHARACTERS FROM MY CHILDHOOD

Mrs. Catherine Smith—My mom. She has loved me every day since I was adopted. She gives me a hug when I feel sad, and she knows how to brighten my day.

Mr. Bob Smith—My dad. He has a big heart. He likes to play with me at the park.

Tim Smith—My older brother. He is the best brother I could ever ask for. We like to go to the library together and play catch at the park.

Kristi Smith—My younger sister. She likes to dance. We play on the swings together.

Birth Mom—I do not remember her much, but I do remember the smell of breakfast foods on her dresses. I also think about the many times we walked to the park to play on the swings.

Birth Dad—I have no memories of him, but I was told his name was Rob, and he was good at fixing cars.

Kelly—Birth sister. I remember feeding her sometimes and listening to her laugh. Another family adopted her after the Smiths adopted me.

Dr. John—My special helper. He has taught my family and me so many things about healing.

Mrs. Beach—My teacher at Vernon Elementary School. She is a great teacher who shows compassion to all her students. She also understands the importance of healing from past hurts.

Kenny Walden—My best friend. We enjoy playing football and riding our bikes together.

Amy Elizabeth—Girl in my class. At first I did not want to be her friend, but then I learned that she is a healing kid too. She grew up to be an author, and she wrote the book *Amy Elizabeth Goes to Play Therapy.*

Mr. Jasper Walden—Kenny's dad. He teaches Kenny and me about football.

Mrs. Shirley Walden—Kenny's mom. She is always smiling. She volunteers at church and always helps those in need.

Baby Jack Walden—Kenny's little brother. He likes to coo and make gurgling sounds.

Mr. Beach—The local baker. He is married to Mrs. Beach and often gives delicious baked goods to her students.

Dorothy—The librarian at the local library. She helps me find books about how to take care of pets.

Sparky—Dorothy's dog. Before I learned about healing, I was not nice to Sparky. Now that I know dogs have feelings too, I am nice to Sparky. I like to pet him and give him dog treats.

Grandpa Shawn Smith—He is a good grandpa who loves football, has a great laugh, and likes to play with his grandchildren.

Grandma Linda Smith—She is a fantastic cook. She takes her grandchildren shopping and has them over for afternoon tea.

Tubby—Best dog ever. He likes to wag his tail and play fetch with us.

Write your name here_____

DRAW A PICTURE OF YOURSELF

Caleb's City Map

Chapter 1

THE BOY WHO HAS
A STORY TO TELL

Hello! My name is Caleb Smith. For those of you that do not know me, it is so nice to meet you. I am also excited to see those of you that already know me from my first book, *A Safe Place for Caleb*. I wrote my first book about living with the Smith family after having many sad and scary things happen in my life before the Smith family adopted me. Although those painful memories happened many years ago, I sometimes still think about them and how important it was for me to heal. I am grown up now with a wonderful wife and two great children. However, things were not always this good. It took a lot of hard work, but as I healed from my past *Hurts*, many things in my life got better.

Now that I am an adult, many people ask me questions about my healing journey as a kid. They ask how I overcame my problems with *Hurts*, anger, attaching (feeling close) to others, fears, and losses from my early years. They wonder how those things troubled me in my daily life when I was younger. People also want to know what was the most helpful during my healing journey.

In order to help answer these questions, I decided to write another book just for you. I will tell you what a typical day looked like for me when I was dealing with *Hurts* and learning to heal. In addition, I will give you some helpful tools for your life if you have had some sad or scary things happen to you. I am so thankful for my family and the help that I received when I was dealing with my past *Hurts*. I am excited to share my *Healing Knowledge* (the good and true things I have learned). Let me start by sharing a little of my story.

When I was four years old, I was taken from my birth mom because she was not able to care for me and I was placed for adoption with the Smith family. My birth mom was white, my birth dad was black, and I am a little of both of them. I wish I had some fun memories of my birth dad, but he did not live with us so I do not really remember him.

I can recall my birth mom and the way she smelled. She would often tell me to be a good boy. My favorite memory is when my birth mom would take me to the park to swing.

While I have a few positive memories of my birth mom, most of my memories of her include yelling, hitting, nasty smells of beer and cigarettes, fears of being left alone in the dark some nights, and sometimes being hungry. I also had a baby sister named Kelly, but she had a different dad. My baby sister was not adopted into the Smith family with me. It makes me sad to remember those experiences.

Many people told me that my life would be better after I went to live with the Smith family. They told me I would be safe in my new home, but these individuals did not totally understand how it feels to be hurt as a child

and the painful memories that stay with you. I am sure you understand what some adults did not know at first—simply removing me from a scary place would not make the fear (and all the problems that came with that) go away. In addition to the painful memories and fear, I always felt a little different than other kids who were not adopted, who did not have lots of *Hurts* when they were younger, who did not have birth parents from different races, or who did not have birth parents that lived separately. For these reasons and many more, the Smith family and I required help in order for me to be able to heal.

The Smith family and I needed a special helper who knew how to help kids like us and the families who love us learn the truth, heal from *Hurts*, and develop an attachment or close feeling to special people in our lives. Thankfully the Smith family found a special helper named Dr. John.

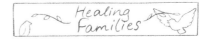

Since I had lots of *Early Hurts* when I was little, I believed many things about life, trust, hope, and people that I later learned were false. Dr. John taught me that *Trauma* (sad and scary experiences) and *Triggers* (reminders of sad and scary experiences) cause *Hurting Beliefs* (false guesses about why *Early Hurts* happened). These *Hurting Beliefs* then cause *Hurting Behaviors* (hurtful things I did to myself and others). After receiving help on my healing journey, the true things that I learned about my early experiences are *Healing Beliefs*. My positive actions and behaviors, as a result of knowing the true *Healing Beliefs*, are *Healing Behaviors*.

When I was younger, I was struggling with many *Hurting Beliefs* and *Hurting Behaviors*. I was often overwhelmed and my past *Hurts* interfered with my day. While working with Dr. John, I identified common attachment challenges contributing to my struggles. Healing is a lot of hard work but it is worth it to be a *Healing Kid*. I healed from my *Early Hurts* and so can you!

My early experiences and work with Dr. John is just the beginning of my life story. If you have past *Hurts*, that is just the beginning of your story too, and you have the power to write healing into your life. Through the years, I learned that everyone (big or small, young or old) is writing the story of his or her life. Even if you do not know it or are not writing words down on paper, you are telling yourself and others about your thoughts, feelings, and experiences and that is a story.

When I was younger, I did not know that I had some choices in how my story turned out. I am here to tell you that you do get to decide some of the things that happen in your story. It is my prayer that you are writing a story of hope and healing instead of just remaining alone with your hurt, fear, and questions. It is not always easy to change a story filled with lots of *Early Hurts* into a happy one, but I know you can write healing into your story if you work hard. While it may seem like I know a lot about healing, this was not always true.

I recently found some of the drawings and writings I created as a kid when I was working on my healing story. Since many people have asked me what a typical day looked like when I was struggling with my *Hurting Beliefs*, I wonder if you would like to go back to when I was learning to heal so that we can write our healing stories together.

In each chapter, I will tell you what my day was like as a kid with the younger version of myself narrating my story, and then I will ask you questions about your experiences. Life is better when you have a friend. Will you be my friend and go on this healing journey with me? It seems like just yesterday that my birthday wish was to have friends and for my *Hurts* to go away. If you are ready to learn more about my childhood and start your own healing story then follow me, I will show you the way.

QUESTIONS

It was helpful for my family to figure out what areas I was struggling with the most. What things do you need help with? (See Common Challenges for Children and Teens, page 74.)

_____

_____

_____

_____

_____

_____

I shared a few of my *Early Hurts* memories. What are your early memories? (See Early Hurts Drawing, page 79.)

_____

_____

_____

_____

_____

_____

Due to my early experiences, I had many *Hurting Beliefs*. What are your *Hurting Beliefs*? (See Hurting Beliefs, page 82.)

_____

_____

_____

_____

_____

_____

I learned to replace the *Hurting Beliefs* with *Healing Beliefs*. What is a *Healing Belief* you would like to remember? (See Healing Beliefs and Healing Behaviors, page 80; Healing Beliefs, page 83.)

_____

_____

_____

_____

_____

When I first started to see Dr. John, I had a lot of fear and anger in my heart. What is in your heart? (See What Is in Your Heart?, page 84.)

_____

_____

_____

_____

_____

_____

DRAW YOURSELF WRITING OR TELLING YOUR STORY

HEALING KNOWLEDGE

Not until we are lost do we begin to understand ourselves.
—Henry David Thoreau

People can heal.

Everyone has a story.

We can share our stories to help us heal.

Common challenges can be overcome.

It is important to ask for help.

Healing Activities for Children and Teens

- Common Challenges for Children and Teens (parent/caregiver component) (page 74)
- Early Hurts Drawing (page 79)
- Healing Beliefs and Healing Behaviors (page 80)
- Hurting Beliefs (page 82)
- Healing Beliefs (page 83)
- What Is in Your Heart? (page 84)

Healing Activities for Parents and Caregivers

- Common Challenges for Parents or Caregivers (page 120)

Chapter 2

THE CASE OF THE MISSING CHOCOLATE CHIPS

Good morning, friends! Welcome to a day in my life.

Today I wake up to the delicious smell of breakfast. I am so excited to find out what mom is cooking that I jump out of bed and land on my school bag. Ouch, sometimes my stuff gets in my way. I grab the school bag and drag it with me as I go to find out what is creating that wonderful smell.

As I enter the kitchen, Mom greets me with a warm "Good morning, Caleb." I notice she is making my favorite breakfast, banana pancakes. Mom makes the pancakes extra special by adding a few chocolate chips on the top in the shape of a smiley face. I sit down at the table as Mom turns to me and asks if I know where the bag of chocolate chips went.

I instantly freeze in a panic. I remember taking the bag of chocolate chips a few days ago and eating them in my room. Before I can even think about it, the words "No, I don't know where they went" slip out of my mouth. As I say this, I think of the empty chocolate chips bag hiding under my bed. Mom says she cannot find the chocolate chips so my pancakes will not have smiley faces on them today.

A few minutes later, I am enjoying my pancakes and I have almost forgotten about the chocolate chips when Mom comes back into the kitchen holding the empty chocolate chips bag. Mom asks me how the bag got under my bed. I get scared that mom will not love me if she knows that I lied when I said I did not know where the chocolate chips went.

I lie again and tell her I do not know how the empty chocolate chips bag got in my room. I know it is wrong to lie, but I would rather lie than have my mom not love me for being a "bad boy." Mom comes over and sits right by me. I am afraid she is going to yell at me and tell me how bad I am. I can feel my heart pounding, and I want to run out of the kitchen. As Mom leans in close, she gently puts her hand on my arm. Mom tells me that when she found the empty chocolate chips bag in my room, she noticed my special food box was empty. She asks me if that is why I stole the chocolate chips. I slowly nod yes.

Mom tells me I will always have enough food at her house, but I remember a time when I was very hungry because I did not have enough food to eat. It is really scary to remember when I needed food and did not have it. In order to make sure I am never without food again, I like to keep food hidden in my room in case I am hungry and need to eat. To help me understand that I will always have food, Mom and I created a special food box.

I keep the special food box in my room and it has snacks like crackers in it that I can eat whenever I need to feel safe. This way I always know that I will have food when I need it. Mom reminds me that if my special food box is empty, all I need to do is tell her and we can go to the store to buy more food. I am very thankful for the food box. Before I had it, I would get in trouble for stealing food and lying about hiding it in my room. Sometimes I would even get up in the middle of the night and go eat food out of the kitchen. Now that I have food in the special food box, I feel safe. However, sometimes when the box is empty, I forget that I can ask my mom for more food. Often the memories of not having enough food just appear in my head without me even trying to think about them, and they are hard to forget. I wonder if I am the only kid that this has happened to.

I am thinking about what foods to buy at the store for my special food box when Mom reminds me that the school bus will be here soon. I quickly finish getting ready for school. I grab my heavy school bag and run out the door. I wish my school bag was lighter so I could run faster. I see the bus coming around the corner. I arrive at the bus stop just in time.

QUESTIONS

My mom keeps me accountable for my actions. To be accountable means to take responsibility for my actions and work on changing them. My goal is to be responsible, respectful, and fun to be around. Who or what keeps you accountable? (See Accountability Paper, page 85.)

_____

_____

_____

_____

_____

_____

I wonder if you ever worry about not having enough food. If you do, maybe you could make a special food box. (See Food Contract, page 87.) What foods would you want to include in your special food box?

_____

_____

_____

_____

_____

_____

I keep my special food box under my bed where it is safe. Where would you put the box?

_____

_____

_____

_____

_____

_____

Have you ever gotten in trouble for lying or stealing? (See Truth Teller Contract, page 89; Stealing Box, page 86.)

_____

_____

_____

_____

_____

_____

DRAW YOURSELF TELLING THE TRUTH

HEALING KNOWLEDGE

Yet is it far better to light the candle than to curse the darkness.

—William Lonsdale Watkinson

You are not alone.

People can change.

Things will get better.

I can be accountable for my actions.

Healing Activities for Children and Teens

- Accountability Paper (page 85)
- Stealing Box (parent/caregiver component) (page 86)
- Food Contract (parent/caregiver component) (page 87)
- Truth Teller Contract (parent/caregiver component) (page 89)

Healing Activities for Parents and Caregivers

- Grounding Techniques (page 121)

Chapter 3

ANGER IS NOT MY FRIEND

When I get to school, my teacher Mrs. Beach tells the class that we will have reading time this morning. I reach for my school bag and find a book to read.

I try to pay attention to the story I am supposed to read so that my parents are proud of me for being a good student. In the story I am reading, the mother and son characters bake muffins together. Reading this story causes me to start thinking about my mom. I worry my mom is upset that I stole the chocolate chips and lied to her.

I am also afraid she will yell at me when I get home. I really want to behave so my parents are not disappointed that I am in their family. Then I wonder if my mom will still want me. Maybe she would like to give me to a different family and choose a new son that is not a bad boy. Suddenly, Mrs. Beach taps me on the shoulder. She reminds me to keep reading. I try to pay attention but it is hard not to get distracted. Finally, reading time is over.

Next, Mrs. Beach asks for a helper to pass out papers. I quickly raise my hand. To my disbelief Mrs. Beach chooses me to be the special helper that gives the other students their papers back. This makes me very excited. I jump out of my seat and almost trip over my school bag. Some of my classmates laugh. Mrs. Beach reminds everyone to be respectful. I really want to make Mrs. Beach proud, so I walk carefully as I complete the special task. I feel successful because Mrs. Beach trusted me to do this important job of giving students their papers back.

After finishing more classwork, it is lunchtime. I eat my lunch fast because after lunch is free time outside. During free time each day, my best friend Kenny and I practice our football skills. Today Amy Elizabeth asks to join us. I am about to say no when I hear Kenny say yes.

Suddenly it feels like someone lit a fire inside of me. How could Kenny do this to me? Kenny and I always practice football together, just the two of us. Now he has replaced me—with a girl! I yell, "Amy Elizabeth is a stupid girl, why would you want her to join us!" Kenny seems surprised by my response. He starts to stick up for Amy Elizabeth. It feels like I am losing my best friend. This makes me so angry that I start calling Amy Elizabeth and Kenny lots of mean names. I swear at them too. Then I see Amy Elizabeth's lunch box. Before I can even think, I am kicking the lunch box and swearing at it.

The yelling and swearing catches Mrs. Beach's attention. I see Mrs. Beach walking over and I know that I will get in trouble. I quickly think up a story about how Kenny was the one that broke Amy Elizabeth's lunch box. I tell Mrs. Beach that it is all Kenny's fault. Mrs. Beach knows that I can be manipulative (by trying to control others) so she does not believe my story. She says my free time outside is over. This is obviously unfair so I complain.

Mrs. Beach explains that I broke three of the school rules: (1) Be friendly to others; (2) No swearing; (3) No hurting people or things (including self and animals). I am still mad, but I do remember learning these school rules as part of the "Be Respectful" school meeting that all the students attended a few weeks ago. Mrs. Beach says I have to spend some time in the "Thinking Corner." The Thinking Corner is where students have to go to sit alone to think about how to make better choices. Mrs. Beach leaves me with the teacher aide in the classroom and she returns outside to be with the other children.

As I stomp to the corner, I kick my school bag and I swear again. I am so angry that as I sit there, all I can think about is how nothing goes my way and I hate everyone, even God.

A few minutes later, I notice a chart on the wall that has a stress scale going from explosive (number five) to calm (number one). I know that I do not get to join the other students again until I am in control of my feelings and body, which is being at a number one on the stress scale. When I first get to the Thinking Corner my anger is at a five. Last time I came to the corner at a five, I could not calm down on my own. Thankfully the teacher aide was there to teach me how to deep breathe. This time I think to myself that I can do the deep breathing by myself.

Maybe you would like to try it with me. I lie on the floor and look at my tummy. I take a deep breath in and watch my belly rise up like a mountain. Then I slowly breathe out and watch my belly sink down like a valley. I do this a few times. It is fun to watch my tummy move up and down when I breathe. I like that I get to control when my body moves up and when it moves down.

After taking a few deep breaths, I am at a three on the stress scale. I am still not all the way to one, but I am doing better. At least I am not as angry as I was before.

Next, I remember that there are worksheets in the Thinking Corner that I can do to help myself calm down. I start with an angry drawing where I draw how mad I am about what happened. Then I fill out worksheets about feelings, staying connected to my body, and thought stopping.

These activities help me release the tension that I feel in my body. As my anger level continues to go down, I am able to think more clearly. I realize I do not actually hate everyone. I just really want people to like me. It hurts when I am afraid the people I care about might not care about me anymore. After I have had some time alone to take some deep breaths and complete some anger and feeling worksheets, my body feels calm. Now when I look at the stress scale I am at a one. Hooray, that means I am ready to join the other students. I show the teacher aide that I have completed the worksheets and tell her that now I am in control of my body. She agrees that I am ready to join the other students.

By this time, Mrs. Beach and the other students are back in the classroom and just about to start math. Sitting in the Thinking Corner was not fun, but at least now it is time for math, my favorite subject. At the bottom of my school bag is the special pencil Dr. John gave me. I take out the pencil and get to work right away solving the math problems. Mrs. Beach asks Kenny to answer question number two. He has the wrong answer.

Next, Mrs. Beach asks me and I have the correct answer. This makes me very happy.

Mrs. Beach is so impressed with my ability to solve the problems that she asks me to help Amy Elizabeth, Kenny, and a few other students. At first, I do not want to help Amy Elizabeth and Kenny because of what happened outside at free time. Before I can say no, I remember rule 1: Be friendly to others. I agree to help them. As I help the other students, I notice I stay calm. Thinking about numbers is easier for me than reading or thinking about other things like feelings. Kenny and Amy Elizabeth both thank me for helping them. This makes me feel very happy and proud. I realize that Amy Elizabeth is actually nice and that Kenny still wants to be my best friend. When I was in the Thinking Corner, all I could think about were all the bad things that had happened today, but now I realize there were some good things too.

QUESTIONS

Sometimes I need to take time to calm down when I am at school. Today, I felt better after having some alone time to take deep breaths and to think. I completed a few worksheets to help my brain and my body calm down. What are things that you can do to calm down at school? Maybe you can complete some of the worksheets I did too. (See Angry Drawing, page 90; Feeling Drawing, page 93; Feeling Emotions, page 95; Stay in Your Body, page 97; Stress Scale, page 100; Thought Stopping, page 99.)

_____

_____

_____

_____

_____

_____

Today, I felt proud when I was the special helper that passed out papers, when I had the correct answer to Mrs. Beach's question, and when I helped the other students solve their math problems. What are some of the things you do at school that make you proud?

_____

_____

_____

_____

_____

_____

I want to work on following the school rules, especially (1) Be friendly to others, (2) No swearing, and (3) No hurting people or things (including self and animals). What are some of the behaviors you need to think about changing to have a better day at school?

_____

_____

_____

_____

_____

_____

I was not a good friend when I broke Amy Elizabeth's lunchbox. What makes a good friend? (See What Makes a Good Friend Checklist, page 101.)

_____

_____

_____

_____

_____

_____

DRAW YOURSELF FEELING CALM

HEALING KNOWLEDGE

The only way to have a friend is to be one.
—Ralph Waldo Emerson

I can learn to trust others.

You can control your thoughts and behaviors.

All people are loved by God.

Feelings are not facts.

Healing Activities for Children and Teens

- Angry Drawing (parent/caregiver component) (page 90)
- Feeling Drawing (page 93)
- Feeling Emotions (page 95)
- Stay in Your Body (page 97)
- Thought Stopping (page 99)
- Stress Scale (page 100)
- What Makes a Good Friend Checklist (page 101)

Healing Activities for Parents and Caregivers

- Coping Skills for Parents and Caregivers (page 122)
- The Five Rs (page 122)

Chapter 4

WHEN THE PAST IS NOT THE PAST

Mrs. Beach announces that school is almost over for today. I start to put my things away and get my school bag ready to go home. Mr. and Mrs. Walden arrive to pick up Kenny a few minutes early because Kenny is going to the dentist. Suddenly, I hear a baby cry. I stop what I am doing, and I look up to see Kenny's baby brother Jack is here.

I watch carefully as Mr. Walden holds Jack and rocks him back and forth to soothe him. Mrs. Walden gives Jack a toy and Mr. Walden makes a soft cooing noise that calms Jack down instantly.

I notice my body feeling jittery, and I want someone to hold me. I try to remember my birth dad, but I cannot picture him or remember what it felt like to be held as a baby. My heart is overwhelmed with sadness as I see Mr. Walden smile at baby Jack because I wish my birth dad had cared for me. Next, Mrs. Walden carries Kenny's school bag for him, and they leave school as a happy family. I really wish I had a loving family with parents who smiled at me, held me, gave me toys, and helped me with things when I was a baby. I wonder why Kenny got a real family right from the start.

I know that the Smiths are a real family, but it does not feel fair that Kenny and baby Jack got to be held by their dad as a baby and were loved from the very beginning. I wish I could go back to being a baby and have things done differently. Why do I think about these things? It makes my heart hurt. My heart feels sad, then mad, then sad all over again.

I am sitting on the floor holding onto my school bag when I feel someone tap my shoulder and say, "Hello, Caleb." I am a bit startled but look up to see my mom. I am glad to see mom because my stomach is churning. I tell Mom I feel sick. She is used to me telling her I have a stomachache. The first time I told Mom my stomach hurt, she thought I had the flu. However, my stomach would hurt almost every day after I was adopted. Then she thought I was making it up to get attention. After she talked to Dr. John about it, she noticed that my stomach hurts and feels nauseous (like I might throw up) when I am *Triggered* (remember a sad or scary memory).

Dr. John taught Mom how to help me listen to my body. As soon as I tell Mom that my stomach hurts, she sits down by me and asks me some questions that help me listen to my body. First, she asks me to describe how my stomach feels. I tell her it feels like a ball is bouncing up and down inside. I also say that my stomach feels sad and forgotten. Next, she asks me what my stomach would say if it could talk. I think about this carefully and decide that my stomach would say it wishes I were held when I was a baby.

Then Mom asks what would make this body part feel better. I respond that I would like a hug. I do not normally like hugs so this response surprises me a little. Mom asks me if she can give me a hug and I say yes. I climb into my mom's lap and she gives me a big hug. Ah, this makes me feel better. It is like my mom is hugging all the jitters out of me.

For those of us that get stomachaches or other aches in our bodies because of bad memories, it is important for us to learn how to listen to our bodies. I am still learning how to do this. You might like to learn how to listen to your body too.

Then I see Mrs. Beach walking over to us. I quickly pull away from mom. I am afraid that Mrs. Beach will tell mom how bad a day I had and then mom will yell at me. Instead, Mrs. Beach hands mom a note. I finish putting my things in my school bag as mom reads the note. Mom looks at me and says, "Wow, Caleb, you worked really hard at school today. Mrs. Beach wrote that you had some good parts of the day and some not so good parts. Let's talk about them on our way to Dr. John's office." I am surprised that mom is proud of me and that Mrs. Beach did not write all bad things about my behavior today. Maybe I am not such a bad boy after all.

Then just before I leave, Mrs. Beach shocks me by giving me a birthday cupcake. It is from her husband's bakery in celebration of my birthday tomorrow. She wishes me a happy birthday. I really like Mrs. Beach, even though I do not want her to know it. It makes me really happy to know that she remembered my birthday is tomorrow. Mom says I can eat the cupcake, and it tastes so delicious.

As I lick the frosting off my fingers, I wonder if I will get a birthday cake tomorrow from the Beach Bakery. Maybe Mom will decide not to get me a cake because I stole chocolate chips and lied to her. Plus with all the things that I have done since the Smiths adopted me, maybe no one in my family will even remember my birthday.

As I get into the car with Mom, I wave to the other students as they get on the bus. Today I am not riding the bus home because I am going to see my special helper Dr. John. On our way to Dr. John's office, Mom and I talk about the good and not so good parts of my day. I bet you can guess what were the good and bad parts. After telling Mom about my day, I think about what we will do at Dr. John's today.

The first time I went to see Dr. John I had a lot of problems and was very anxious about meeting him. You see, when children like you and me have had sad and scary things happen to us when we were younger, we need help to heal. I have learned that *Hurts* do not heal on their own even if you try extra hard to just forget everything. Dr. John works with children and their families that have issues with attachment (problems trusting people) and *Trauma* (sad or scary experiences that caused *Hurts*). Some days I work with Dr. John alone for individual or play therapy, and other days my whole family comes to family therapy. Not too long ago, I joined a group for group therapy with other *Healing Kids* just like me.

I am excited to see what we will do today because Dr. John has lots of fun ways to help kids like you and me. I like Dr. John but sometimes I still wonder if I can trust anyone, especially when people like the Smiths get mad over little things like chocolate chips. It sure is hard to have issues with attachment.

We arrive at Dr. John's office a few minutes early. I see the food store next to Dr. John's office. That reminds me I need to refill my special food box.

Therefore, I ask Mom if we can go to the store. She agrees so we pick out some crackers, fruit snacks, and granola bars to put in my food box at home. I am excited because the granola bars we found have a few little chocolate chips in them.

Hopefully, now I will not steal chocolate chips from the Smiths' kitchen. As we are about to leave, I notice some lunch boxes. After having some time to calm down in the Thinking Corner, I regret breaking Amy Elizabeth's lunch box. I am standing frozen in front of the lunch boxes remembering what happened at school today when mom hurries me out of the store and into Dr. John's office.

QUESTIONS

When I was *Triggered* (reminded of my sad and scary experiences), my stomach hurt. Are there places in your body that hurt when you are *Triggered*? (See Listening to My Body, page 102.)

_____

_____

_____

_____

_____

_____

Sometimes I tell myself I am a bad boy or that I am not good enough to be loved. It is called *Negative Self-Talk* when you have negative thoughts that you tell yourself. What *Negative Self-Talk* do you tell yourself? (See What Are Your Negative Self-Talk Triggers?, page 104.)

_____

_____

_____

_____

_____

_____

I was *Triggered* when I saw baby Jack being cared for by his dad at school. What *Triggers* you? (See What Are Your Triggers?, page 105.)

_____

_____

_____

_____

_____

_____

I feel like I missed out on the best parts of being a baby. I wish I was held more as a baby. What do you wish you had as a baby? (See Developmental Lost Experiences, page 106.)

_____

_____

_____

_____

_____

_____

DRAW SOMEONE CARING FOR YOU

HEALING KNOWLEDGE

The darkest hour is just before the dawn.

—Thomas Fuller

Healing takes time.

I am deserving of love and kindness.

Communication is important.

People care about me.

Healing Activities for Children and Teens

- Listening to My Body (page 102)
- What Are Your Negative Self-Talk Triggers? (page 104)
- What Are Your Triggers? (page 105)
- Developmental Lost Experiences (parent/caregiver component) (page 106)

Healing Activities for Parents and Caregivers

- Helpful Affirmations for Parents or Caregivers (page 123)
- Triggers Checklist for Parents or Caregivers (page 124)

Chapter 5

HEALING IS HARD WORK

When I arrive at Dr. John's office, I go to the group therapy room. I sit down at a table by some of the other children. Then Dr. John walks in. I look up and am shocked because standing next to Dr. John is Amy Elizabeth. Dr. John introduces Amy Elizabeth. I cannot believe that Amy Elizabeth has past *Hurts* that need healing just like me. I think back to earlier today when I did not like Amy Elizabeth because she wanted to be Kenny's friend. When I look at Amy Elizabeth, I can see that she is scared. I remember how scared I was when I first came to therapy. I also think of the things about a person that make a good friend.

I decide I want to be a good friend to Amy Elizabeth so I ask her to sit by me. She looks happy to know someone. Dr. John asks us all to tell our names to Amy Elizabeth and share a little about ourselves. I learn that Amy Elizabeth is really good at art.

Next, Dr. John tells us that this week we will be making a Grief Box.

At first I said, "What is a grief box?" Once Dr. John explained how to make a grief box, I was excited to start on the project. I will tell you all about how to make a grief box in case you want to make one too. A grief box is a place to keep reminders of important things from my past that I am working on healing. It is also where I keep reminders of the many things that I lost as a result of those sad and scary things that happened to me in my early years. I use a big shoebox to make my grief box. I write the words GRIEF and LOSSES in big letters. I then paint the box with my favorite colors. Next, I write words and draw pictures of the things that I feel super-sad about. I also add the things and people that I lost in my early years. Dr. John says we can put things from home in the box too. Right away I know what I want to put in my grief box. It is a small frog stuffed animal that I had when I came to live with the Smith family when they adopted me. My mom has been keeping it in a safe place for me, but now I will put it in my grief box as a reminder of the fun times that I lost before I was adopted.

When Dr. John first started talking about losses, I did not totally understand what I had lost. I thought losing something meant I could go find it—like when I lost my watch at school. Now I know that you can have lost experiences with people or feelings of safety that cannot just be picked up from where they were hiding. Today Dr. John asks us to share with the group of kids some of the things that we have put in our grief boxes.

When it is my turn, I tell the group that my Dad told me once that he felt like he lost out on my early years because he did not get to change my diapers. I think diapers are stinky so I laughed so hard when I heard what Dad said. While it is funny that my dad wanted to change my diaper, sometimes I think it would have been nice to have him in my early years to take care of me. I show the group the picture I drew of my dad changing my diaper because I did not get to have this experience.

I also show the group a picture I drew of my birth mom and my baby sister Kelly. I tell the other kids that even though my birth mom and baby sister Kelly are both alive, they are lost to me because I do not see them anymore. I still miss them so I put this picture in my grief box too. Amy Elizabeth shares that she lost her ability to feel safe with people. I feel this way sometimes too.

After everyone has an opportunity to share some of the losses in their grief box, Dr. John tells us that group is over for today. While it is time for some of the children to go home, I have family therapy after group today. I notice that Amy Elizabeth goes into the play therapy room with her special helper so it must be her day for individual therapy. I see Mom, Dad, Tim (my older brother), and Kristi (my younger sister) waiting for me when I come out of the group room. It means a lot to me to have everyone in my family here.

Today in family therapy I show my family one of my favorite healing activities. It is called a *Safe Tree House*. I have been using it for a while and it

really helps me. One of the cool things about a *Safe Tree House* is you can make it lots of different ways. You can build it using cards and paper, draw it, or even think about it in your mind.

I made this *Safe Tree House* using cards and paper to represent the *Safe Tree House* that I created in my mind. First, I explain to my family that the purpose of the *Safe Tree House* is so that the parts of me that got hurt when I was younger, which I call my younger *Hurt Self*, can have a place to heal.

My mom says she remembers some of the *Hurts* I shared with her when I filled out a worksheet called Writing My Story a few weeks ago. She tells me she is glad that I am able to have a *Safe Tree House* to heal my *Hurt Selves*.

Dr. John helps me explain that sometimes when we are hurt, we leave that *Hurt Self* behind. It is then important for us to find our *Hurt Self* so we can learn to heal, trust, and love again. Before I was adopted, someone hurt my body when I was four years old so I have my four-year-old *Hurt Self* go into my *Safe Tree House*. It may sound weird but I feel so much better when I have a memory or scary thought and I can have my scared *Hurt Self* go to the *Safe Tree House*.

I pretend that special angels rescue me from the place where I was hurt or where I watched other people get hurt. The angels pick me up and carry my *Hurt Self* to the *Safe Tree House*. Instead of having memories of my hurt four-year-old self being alone and afraid in the place where my body was hurt, my *Hurt Self* now lives in the *Safe Tree House*. When my *Hurt Self* lives in the *Safe Tree House* instead of my sad and scary memories, my *Hurt Self* can heal and grow up to the age that I am now.

It feels so good to tell my family about the healing my *Hurt Self* gets inside the *Safe Tree House*. I want everyone to live in a place of healing instead of a place full of *Hurts*. Dr. John reminds my family, "It is time for the pain to stop!" I agree, and I am guessing you agree too.

After I show my family my *Safe Tree House*, Dr. John tells us today we will be working on *Triggers* (the reminders of the sad and scary things that happen in our lives) as a family. Dr. John asks each person to share ways that he or she felt *Triggered* in the last week. By sharing our *Triggers*, we all think of ways to help deal with future *Triggers*. I am surprised to learn that my family members can have *Triggers* too. I wonder if everyone has *Triggers*.

When it is my turn to share, I tell my family that I felt *Triggered* when I saw Kenny's dad take care of baby Jack. I was *Triggered* because as a baby I did not always get what I needed. When I saw baby Jack getting his needs met, I started to wonder why some babies get their needs met but I did not. As I tell the story, I realize that believing I did not deserve to have my needs met as a baby is a *Hurting Belief*. I want to replace this false belief with a *Healing Belief*. I think about how I deserve good things. I share this *Healing Belief* with my family. They are proud of me for replacing my *Hurting Belief* with a *Healing Belief*. We continue to share our *Triggers* as a family. It is nice to think of *Healing Beliefs* for each other. At the end of our family therapy session, Dr. John asks my family and me to think of positive things to say to each other

throughout the week. Then we say goodbye to Dr. John. He tells me, "You worked very hard today Caleb, see you next week."

QUESTIONS

I made a *Safe Tree House* for my *Hurt Self*. I also wrote about my *Hurt Self*. Do you have a *Hurt Self* too? (See Creating Your Own Safe Place, page 107; Writing My Story, page 112.)

_____

_____

_____

_____

_____

_____

I feel like I lost out on not being cared for by a dad as a baby. What are some of the things that you lost from having sad or scary things happen to you? (See Instructions for Creating a Grief Box, page 110; A Time to Remember: Grief and Losses, page 110; My Grief Box, page 111.)

_____

_____

_____

_____

_____

_____

It is important to tell our families and ourselves nice things. What nice things can you tell yourself and your family? (See Positive Things to Tell Yourself, page 114.)

_____

_____

_____

_____

_____

_____

DRAW YOURSELF HEALING

HEALING KNOWLEDGE

The real voyage of discovery consists not in seeking new landscapes, but in having new eyes.

—Marcel Proust

Healing is hard work but it is worth it.

Families provide support.

Love is to be experienced and shared.

I deserve good things.

Healing Activities for Children and Teens

- Creating Your Own Safe Place (page 107)
- Instructions for Creating a Grief Box (page 110)
- A Time to Remember: Grief and Losses (page 110)
- My Grief Box (page 111)
- Writing My Story (page 112)
- Positive Things to Tell Yourself (page 114)

Healing Activities for Parents and Caregivers

- Family Bonding Activities (page 126)

Chapter 6

THE SHADOW IN
THE CORNER?

As we are leaving Dr. John's office, I see Amy Elizabeth is getting ready to go home too. I am still surprised that Amy Elizabeth was in my group today. I learned she is actually a fun girl, and she has had sad and scary things happen to her just like me. Suddenly, I have an idea. I remember that I have some money in my school bag. My mom gave it to me in case of an emergency and right now I have an emergency. I grab the money and I am about to run to the store, but first I quickly tell Mom my plan. She smiles at me and says that I have an excellent plan. She walks with me to the store. I run to the lunch boxes and pick out a pretty pink one with sparkles. We buy it and go back to Dr. John's office.

Amy Elizabeth is just about to leave. I yell, "Wait!" She looks startled but waits. I run to her and give her the new pink lunch box with sparkles. I apologize for breaking her old lunch box and calling her names. Amy Elizabeth says, "You are forgiven."

It feels so good to be forgiven. I start thinking of other things in my life I would like to be forgiven for when Mom comes over to me and tells me it is time to go. Today has been a long day since I went to school, group therapy, and family therapy. Therapy is hard work, but it is worth it.

Since therapy is such hard work, my family usually tries to relax the rest of the night. It is important to give our bodies and minds time to rest after therapy. We learned that it is too overwhelming to plan other events or spend time with friends on therapy nights. It is also important to check in with yourself to see if you need to rest, relax, or release your energy. Then tell your parent or caregiver what you need. Today, I tell my mom that I need to release energy. She suggests we go to the park for a short time on our way home.

I love going to the park. I feel as if all my worries are washed away when I soar through the air on the swings. On our way to the park, I can feel my energy bubbling inside of me wanting to escape. As soon as Mom parks the car, I jump out and run towards the swings. I get to the swings and see a tall man nearby. Maybe he will give me a push on the swings so I can go really high. As I start running towards the man, I hear my mom yell, "Caleb, remember our safety rules." This causes me to stop. In a flash an image of a mean scary man that once hurt me comes into my mind. I start running away from the man and towards my mom. By the time I get to the swings, I feel out of breath.

Then Mom pushes me high on the swings and for those few minutes that I am soaring through the air, my worries disappear.

As we walk back to the car to go home, I see Dorothy walking her dog Sparky. Dorothy works at our local library. Last year when I was really struggling with a lot of *Hurts* in my life, I was mean to Sparky. I did not know that dogs needed love just like me. Dorothy gave me some books and I learned all about how to take care of pets. Now Sparky and I are friends. I love to pet him and watch his cute little tail wag. He gets excited to see me and sometimes even licks my face. I hope that someday I can have a dog of my very own.

I want to go over and say hi to them but I remember that it is often hard for me to be around people on the nights that I have therapy. Dr. John says this happens when we are remembering and healing our past *Hurts*. On days when I have more hurting memories, I feel more *Triggered* and have a difficult time getting along with people. I just wave to them as we walk by. Dorothy knows that Friday is therapy night so she will understand.

When we get home, dad has pizza ready for us. I quickly toss my school bag into my room and get ready to eat dinner as a family. Today it is Kristi's turn to say the prayer. She thanks God for our food and healing. I am really excited to eat the pizza until I put it in my mouth. It is too hot and an olive gets stuck to my tongue. The texture of the food bothers me because the olive is slippery and slimy. I feel like I am going to gag. I quickly take a drink of water. Mom helps me pick off all the olives from my pizza and I wait for it to cool down. I cannot explain it but sometimes certain textures or temperatures bother me.

After dinner, I take a bath before we watch a family movie. I usually find it relaxing to snuggle under a blanket and watch a movie at home. Today I look out the window at the dark night sky. I notice my body starts to feel different. It is weird because I cannot feel parts of my body while at the same time other parts of me want to run away. I quickly find a blanket, curl up into a ball, and hide. I am scared, but I am not sure what I want to hide from or why. Mom and Dad must have noticed me hiding under the blanket because they come over and sit by me. They tell me I am safe, and they are here with me. I poke my head out from the blanket. I see that Mom and Dad are here with me and that I am safe. Dad asks if I would like to pick out the movie we watch. I do.

After the movie, it is bedtime. Nighttime is the hardest part of the day for me. This could be because it is dark outside, the house is quiet, or I have more time to think about things. I tend to think about things that happened to me before the Smiths adopted me.

As I am climbing into my bed, I see something that frightens me. It is a dark image in the corner. I can feel the fear inside my body.

Normally, hugging my teddy bear gives me comfort, but as I look around the room, I cannot find my teddy bear. Now I am sad, too. My heart aches as it fills with sadness and fear. I am afraid to go to sleep without my teddy bear because I do not want to dream about scary things. Suddenly, I hear a noise behind me. This causes me to jump and my heart is pounding so hard it might burst from my chest. I turn around to see my brother, Tim. Oh, good. It is not another monster, it is just Tim. I explain to him that I cannot go to bed because there is a monster in the corner. Tim is really brave so he goes to the corner and looks for the monster. I turn away as Tim reaches near the lamp to grab the monster. I hear Tim say, "Ah ha, I have captured the monster." I turn to look expecting to see a big ugly monster when I see Tim holding my school bag.

I then remember that when I had gotten home earlier today, I put my school bag in the corner. Now I can see that the light coming in from my window creates a strange shadow on my wall. Next, my mom comes in to say goodnight and she is carrying my teddy bear. Relief floods me. You can probably understand how glad I was to see that I did not have a monster in my room, and I had my teddy bear to hug.

At this point, I still do not want to go to bed. I am afraid that I will have bad dreams. When I complain about having to go to bed, Mom reminds me that I have the power to change any bad dream. Once when I had a bad dream about a snake chasing me in the woods, I woke up and Mom showed me how to rewrite my dream. When I rewrote my dream, I was a knight in shining armor carrying a powerful sword, and I scared the snake away. As I remember this, I feel more in control.

Mom reads me a story, I turn on my nightlight, and I hug my bear. As I lay in bed, I remember that tomorrow is my birthday. I imagine a wonderful birthday party with lots of people celebrating as I drift off to sleep.

QUESTIONS

I felt relieved when Amy Elizabeth forgave me. Has there been a time in your life when you asked for forgiveness? Is there someone you would like to ask to forgive you?

_____

_____

_____

_____

_____

Playing on the swings helps me release extra energy and calm down. What helps you release energy and calm down?

_____

_____

_____

_____

_____

I get scared at nighttime by the dark and fear of bad dreams. What scares you at nighttime? Do you ever have bad dreams? (See Changing Your Dreams, page 115.)

_____

_____

_____

_____

_____

DRAW YOURSELF HAVING A GOOD DREAM

HEALING KNOWLEDGE

That which we persist in doing becomes easier, not that the task itself has become easier, but that our ability to perform it has improved.

—Ralph Waldo Emerson

Forgiveness is powerful.

Know your limits and practice boundaries.

I can heal one day at a time.

Healing Activities for Children and Teens

- Changing Your Dreams (page 115)

Healing Activities for Parents and Caregivers

- Sensory Issues (page 128)

Chapter 7

HEALING KIDS CELEBRATE

When I wake up the next morning, I can tell I slept in late, but I am so excited because it is my birthday today! Only my dad is home when I get up so I think that my family must have forgotten about me. The other option is that my mom is still mad at me and does not love me anymore because of my misbehaviors yesterday. I am feeling sad and alone when Dad says that we need to complete some errands.

We get in the car and while we are driving I realize we are not going to do errands. Instead, we are on our way to my grandparents' house. We arrive at the house and I see lots of cars outside. I wonder what could be happening. I run to the door and open it. When I enter into the house, my

family and friends greet me. They say, "Surprise" and "Happy birthday, Caleb." I feel so loved and excited that all these people came to celebrate my birthday with me. This is the best birthday ever.

After we play some games and eat lunch, Mom says she has a special dessert. Then I see Mr. Beach from the Beach Bakery carrying a huge cake. Wow! The cake even has chocolate chips in it, my favorite. I can hardly believe that Mr. and Mrs. Beach delivered such a delicious cake for my party. My mom puts candles on the cake and everyone sings a birthday song for me. I blow out the candles as I make a wish. My wish is that every day would be as special as this one.

So many people surround me that love and care about me and it feels great!

Just when I think this day could not get any better, Dad announces it is time for presents. I sit down by beautifully wrapped presents. It still surprises me to get gifts on my birthday because I did not get many gifts in my early years. The gift boxes look so pretty, I almost do not want to open them. Of course I also want to know what I have been given so I open the presents. From Kenny I get a pirate ship. Grandma and Grandpa give me a new ball. Kristi made me a picture frame with a photograph of our family inside. Just as I think I have finished opening all the gifts, I hear a barking sound. Hmmm…that seems odd. Then dad walks into the room with a dog. I recognize this dog. It is Tubby from the Animal Rescue Center.

I run superfast to Tubby and give him a big hug. Dad says our family has adopted Tubby. I am overwhelmed with excitement.

I have been wishing for a dog for a long time. When I asked for a dog in the past, Mom and Dad said I was not ready to take care of one. They explained that I had a lot of healing work to do before I could be responsible for a dog. This made me work extra hard during my time with Dr. John, and I read so many books from Dorothy about how to take care of pets. I even volunteered at the Animal Rescue Center with Tim where we took dogs for walks and brushed their fur.

The Animal Rescue Center is where I met Tubby. Tubby reminds me of myself. Tubby and I both needed rescuing and a family to care for us. Now I get to be that family for Tubby. I already know that we will be best friends. I am so proud that Mom and Dad think I am ready to take care of a dog. This just shows that I am making a lot of good changes in my life. I look around the room and see my friends and family smiling at me. Even though some days I still remember my past *Hurts*, I am thankful for days like this. I am so glad I am a *Healing Kid*! What a wonderful celebration.

I hope that you work hard to share your healing story and become a *Healing Kid* too! I'll be cheering for you.

Your friend,

Caleb

Caleb

QUESTIONS

At first, I thought my mom forgot my birthday or was mad at me. Do you ever have the wrong thoughts about what someone else is thinking?

_____

_____

_____

_____

_____

It can be helpful to recognize the progress you have made along your healing journey. Are you wondering what progress you have made? (See Common Challenges for Children and Teens Reassessed, page 116; What Is in Your Heart Now?, page 117.) Compare your current results/drawing with the ones you did before.

_____

_____

_____

_____

_____

It is important to celebrate accomplishments and healing from past *Hurts*. How do you like to celebrate?

_____

_____

_____

_____

_____

_____

Healing Kids work hard to heal from their past *Hurts*. I am a *Healing Kid*. You are a *Healing Kid* too. What does it look like to be a *Healing Kid*? (See Healing Award, page 118.)

_____

_____

_____

_____

_____

_____

How do you think my life turned out? You can read the book *A Safe Place for Caleb* (Chara and Chara 2005) to learn more about my life.

DRAW YOURSELF AS A *HEALING KID*

HEALING KNOWLEDGE

*There is no value in life except what you choose to place
upon it and no happiness in any place except what you
bring to it yourself.*

—Henry David Thoreau

Healing is a journey, not a destination.

Celebrate accomplishments and milestones.

Healing Activities for Children and Teens

- Common Challenges for Children and Teens Reassessed (parent/caregiver component) (page 116)
- What Is in Your Heart Now? (page 117)
- Healing Award (page 118)

Healing Activities for Parents and Caregivers

- Common Challenges for Parents or Caregivers Reassessed (page 129)
- Celebrate Healing (page 130)

PART 2

ACTIVITIES AND ASSESSMENTS

HEALING ACTIVITIES AND ASSESSMENTS FOR CHILDREN AND TEENS

ILLUSTRATIONS BY TASHA A. LEHNER

Common Challenges for Children and Teens

	Symptoms	None		A Little		A Lot		All the Time	
1	Lying								
2	Stealing								
3	Food issues								
4	Anger								
5	Manipulation								
6	Troubles with friends								
7	Difficulty following rules								
8	Nighttime/sleep issues								
9	Grief/sadness								
10	Sensory issues								
11	Fear								
12	Safety								
13	Lack of trust								
14	Triggers								
15	Troubles with feelings								
16	Body aches/pains								

While thinking of a regular week, rate how often the common challenges occur. The child/teen can mark in the white space and the parent/caregiver can mark in the shaded area for each symptom.

None – does not occur
A Little – occurs 1–3 days of the week
A Lot – occurs 4–6 days of the week
All the Time – occurs every day, maybe even multiple times a day

For the child/teen:
List the two common challenges you are most ready to work on:

_____

_____

List the two common challenges you are most afraid of or concerned about working on:

_____

_____

Child/teen: _____ Date: _____

Parent/caregiver: _____ Date: _____

Scoring the Common Challenges

After completing the checklist, identify the child's top four common challenges—starting with the ones with the highest level of occurrence. We recommend that you also give consideration to additional assessment scores and reports of challenges (from child/teen, parent/caregiver, teacher, counselor) before determining which common challenges should be focused on. We suggest that you do not work on more than four challenges at a time or the healing process can become too overwhelming for all family members. Once improvement is noted with one of the common challenges, another can be worked on. It is important to work on the common challenges at the pace of the child and family. Working too fast can cause families to feel lost in the healing process.

Below is a list of activities included in this book that can be used when working on common challenge areas. The activities are listed in the categories that they are most related to; some activities can be utilized to address multiple common challenges. Please consider using additional resources for working on these common challenges.

Activities Related to Common Challenges

Lying:

Truth Teller Contract (page 89)

Accountability Paper (page 85)

Stealing:

Stealing Box (page 86)

Food Issues:

Food Contract (page 87)

Anger:

Angry Drawing (page 90)

Stress Scale (page 100)

Feeling Emotions (page 95)

Manipulation:

Accountability Paper (page 85)

Thought Stopping (page 99)

Troubles with Friends:

Thought Stopping (page 99)

What Makes a Good Friend Checklist (page 101)

Difficulty following Rules:

Accountability Paper (page 85)

Nighttime/Sleep Issues:

Changing Your Dreams (page 115)

Grief/Sadness:

Developmental Lost Experiences (page 106)

Instructions for Creating a Grief Box (page 110)

A Time to Remember: Grief and Losses (page 110)

My Grief Box (page 111)

Sensory Issues:

Sensory Issues (page 128)

Fear:

Early Hurts Drawing (page 79)

What is in Your Heart? (page 84)

Stay in Your Body (page 97)

Safety:

Creating Your Own Safe Place (page 107)

Writing My Story (page 112)

Lack of Trust:

Healing Beliefs and Healing Behaviors (page 80)

Hurting Beliefs (page 82)

Healing Beliefs (page 83)

Creating Your Own Safe Place (page 107)

Triggers:

What Are Your Negative Self-Talk Triggers? (page 104)

What Are Your Triggers? (page 105)

Positive Things to Tell Yourself (page 114)

Troubles with Feelings:

What Is in Your Heart? (page 84)

Feeling Drawing (page 93)

Feeling Emotions (page 95)

Body Aches/Pains:

Feeling Emotions (page 95)

Listening to My Body (page 102)

Caleb's Early Hurts
Drawing Example

SIGHTS

I saw the police at my house

SOUNDS

I heard storms when I was alone

SMELLS

I smelled rotten trash/rubbish and cigarettes

FEELINGS

I felt scared

_____'s Early Hurts Drawing

Write your name here

Instructions: Draw and write memories of sights, sounds, smells, and feelings of your early years of *Hurts* and *Trauma* experiences.

SIGHTS	SOUNDS
_____	_____

SMELLS	FEELINGS
_____	_____

Healing Beliefs

I have a choice to do right or wrong, to smile or frown, and to laugh or cry
I have a voice. I will use my strong voice today
My needs do matter and I can learn how to get them met in a safe way
Feelings can be scary at times but feelings can never cause death
Some people are trustworthy, and some are not. I can learn how to tell the
*   difference*
I deserve to be loved and love the ones who love me
Why all this happened had nothing to do with me
I am a good kid
I can heal one day at a time
I can use my Safe Tree House when I am afraid
God loves me and hurts that I was hurt

Healing Behaviors

Tell the truth
Do not steal
Be kind to animals
Don't interrupt when others are talking
Say kind words to others
Show respect to others
Don't be a show-off and put others down
Look for the good and not the bad in others
Be a good friend
Help other people
Show care and love to others
Try to do the right thing
Apologize for bad behavior
Ask for forgiveness if my actions hurt others
Act appropriately with different kinds of people (keep proper boundaries)
I do to others as I would have them do to me
Act the way God would have me act

(Adapted from Chara and Chara 2005)

Caleb's Hurting Beliefs Example

Reminders of sad or scary experiences (*Triggers*): Remembering my birth family.

Sad or scary event that happened (*Trauma* or *Early Hurts*): Being separated from my birth mom and baby sister Kelly.

Lies or false guesses believed (*Hurting Beliefs*): I am a bad boy and no one will ever love me.

Actions that cause harm to self or others (*Hurting Behaviors*): Push people away.

Caleb's Healing Beliefs Example

Reminders of sad or scary experiences (*Triggers*): Remembering my birth family.

Sad or scary event that happened (*Trauma* or *Early Hurts*): Being separated from my birth mom and baby sister Kelly.

Good and true beliefs (*Healing Beliefs*): I deserve a family, and I am worthy of being loved.

Good and true behaviors (*Healing Behaviors*): Connect with others.

_____'s **Hurting Beliefs**

Write your name here

Instructions: After you have been *Triggered* by *Early Hurts* and engaged in inappropriate thoughts or behaviors, this worksheet can be helpful to facilitate healing thoughts and behaviors. Start by completing the first box and work your way down. Remember, *Trauma* behaviors are usually driven by fear.

Triggers, *Trauma*, and *Early Hurts* create *Hurting Beliefs* that lead to *Hurting Behaviors*.

Reminders of sad or scary experiences (*Triggers*):

Sad or scary event that happened (*Trauma* or *Early Hurts*):

Lies or false guesses believed (*Hurting Beliefs*):

Actions that cause harm to self or others (*Hurting Behaviors*):

_____'s **Healing Beliefs**

Write your name here

Instructions: After you have been *Triggered* by *Early Hurts* and engaged in inappropriate thoughts or behaviors, this worksheet can be helpful to facilitate healing thoughts and behaviors. Start by completing the first box and work your way down. Remember, *Trauma* behaviors are usually driven by fear.

Triggers, *Trauma*, and *Early Hurts* can be **changed** with help through *Healing Beliefs* and *Healing Behaviors*.

Reminders of sad or scary experiences (*Triggers*):

Sad or scary event that happened (*Trauma* or *Early Hurts*):

Good and true beliefs (*Healing Beliefs*):

Good and true behaviors (*Healing Behaviors*):

What Is in Your Heart?

Choose a color for each emotion. Color how your heart feels. You can also draw or write memories that are in your heart.

Color the box that matches the emotion:

- ☐ Anger
- ☐ Fear
- ☐ Loneliness
- ☐ Happiness
- ☐ Sadness

Accountability Paper

Instructions: Following misbehaviors, complete the Accountability Paper and talk with an adult about the contents of the paper. (Activity adapted from Bruce Buchanan.)

Goal: Be responsible, respectful, and fun to be around.

What did I do wrong?

List the people affected (include self).

How did my behavior affect others?

What should I do next time? Explain how you will do it differently.

Stealing Box

Instructions: Create a Stealing Box with an adult. Put non-edible items into the Stealing Box. Once a day, you can secretly steal an item from the Stealing Box when no one is watching you. By creating a Stealing Box, you agree to only steal from the box and not from anywhere else. You are able to keep the items you steal from the box. However, if you do steal from somewhere else, you must return all items previously stolen from the Stealing Box back to the Stealing Box. At the end of each day, talk to an adult about why you stole the item and how you felt before and after stealing.

Note to Parents/Caregivers: Trust us, this activity actually helps prevent future stealing by eliminating the thrill of stealing and allowing for hurting children/teens to express their desire to get their needs met from previous hurting experiences. (Activity adapted from Bruce Buchanan.)

What would you put in your Stealing Box? Write or draw what you would put in your Stealing Box.

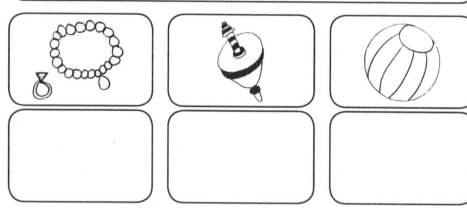

I agree not to steal from anywhere else in or out of the home. I will remember that if I do steal from somewhere other than the Stealing Box, I must return ALL items back to the Stealing Box. I agree to only take one turn a day with the Stealing Box, and I will talk to an adult at the end of each day about my stealing feelings.

Child/teen signature: _____ Date: _____

Food Contract

Instructions: Create a contract for home and/or school where food items (usually non-perishable in bedroom or perishable for school bags) can be kept in an agreed-upon location for a specified timeframe (recommend 3 to 6 months and reassess).

This contract is an agreement that _____ is allowed to keep the following items in an agreed upon location for a specified timeframe.

Items: _____

_____

_____

Location: _____

Timeframe: _____

Parent/caregiver signature: _____ Date: _____

I agree not to take food from others, hoard food, or hide food for later. I will talk to adults about concerns over food or when I need something. I will always have enough food.

Child/teen signature: _____ Date: _____

Truth Teller Contract Instructions

Lying is a common problem with children/teens who have had *Relational Injury*. As a result, the Truth Teller Contract is designed to reduce the frequency of lying and eventually eliminate lying. This is accomplished by allowing the child/teen to lie for 30 seconds before he/she is held accountable for his/her behavior. As the lying decreases, so does the allotted lying period.

Instructions for child/teen: You have 30 seconds to tell all the lies you want to tell. Following this allowed lying period, you must tell the truth. If you do not tell the truth after the allowed lying time, then a predetermined consequence that you and your parent/caregiver decide will take place.

Parents/caregivers: By allowing the child/teen to lie, followed by being required to tell the truth, the child/teen learns to separate fact from falsehood and that there is a time for telling the truth. While this concept may seem crazy to some, this activity is adapted from Bruce Buchanan's 30 Second Lie Rule Technique and Chara and Chara's (2005) The Lying Period. Remember, the goal of the activity is to separate facts from falsehoods and reduce lying with the end goal of eliminating the desire to lie. (*Note:* This activity is not recommended for children 5 years old or younger because they do not usually understand why they are lying.)

Truth Teller Contract

This contract is an agreement that _____
will tell the Truth!

I admit that I have a problem with not telling the truth at times, and I agree to work hard at becoming a **Truth Teller**.

In a situation where I typically lie, I will be given 30 seconds of lying time before I must check myself to see if I am lying. After the 30 seconds of lying time, I must tell the listener the truth to avoid having a consequence. As I get better with truth telling by successfully telling the truth after the allowed 30 second lying period multiple times, I will begin using a 15 second lying period, then 5 second lying period, and then I will only be given a prompt like "You are on the clock now" or "I am listening for your Truth."

After the lying period has ended or the prompt has been given, I agree to the following consequence if I do not tell the truth and continue lying.

Consequence for lying after time period/prompts: _____

_____

I also agree that I will complete an Accountability Paper (page 85) for lying if asked.

Child/teen signature: _____ Date: _____

Parent/caregiver signature: _____ Date: _____

Angry Drawing

Instructions for the adult demonstrating the Angry Drawing

Children and teens can complete Angry Drawings to assist with the identification and healthy expression of anger by using crayons and a thin type of paper (e.g. construction paper, sugar paper). Before a child/teen completes the activity, a trusted adult should first demonstrate an Angry Drawing in order to model healthy anger expressions.

1. Arrange several pieces of paper in one stack. The top page of paper will be used to begin the activity. Gather crayons to use also.

2. Tell the child/teen that lots of people have things that make them angry, and creating an Angry Drawing is a way to help express and deal with those feelings.

3. Explain that people can write or draw a picture of what makes them feel angry.

4. Demonstrate writing or drawing a picture of an angry feeling (usually about friends or family). (*Note:* It is recommended to use an example not referencing the child/teen that will be completing the activity.)

5. After writing or drawing a picture of an angry feeling, choose a crayon color to represent anger (usually red or black).

6. Place the crayon in your fist and rapidly color all over the angry words or drawing. (*Note:* The paper on the top of the stack will usually tear due to the force of pressing down so hard. This causes the angry coloring to continue onto the sheet of paper under the original writing or drawing.)

7. Make positive statements after completing the angry coloring. Examples: "Look how much anger I had." "I can release my anger without hurting anyone or anything." "I feel better now."

8. Ask the child/teen if he or she would like to do the Angry Drawing activity. If so, walk the child/teen through the steps for creating an Angry Drawing.

Angry Drawing

Instructions for the adult to give to the child/ teen completing the Angry Drawing

Start by helping the child/teen gather the necessary supplies (stack of paper and crayons—same as used for the demonstration).

1. Write or draw what makes you angry.

2. Choose a crayon color to represent your anger.

3. Color over the angry words or drawing to get your anger out.

4. Notice how you feel when you do this activity and look at your Angry Drawing. (Adult and child/teen can discuss child/teen's reactions and comments throughout this activity.)

5. Remember the Anger Rules: Do not hurt self, others, or things!

Caleb's Feeling Drawing Examples

I feel _____ Fearful _____

I feel _____ Hurt _____

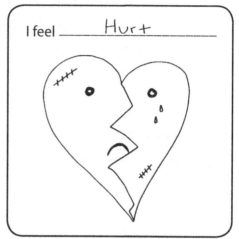

I feel _____ Hopeful _____

I feel _____ Successful _____

_____'s Feeling Drawing

Instructions: Identify a feeling. Draw what this feeling looks like or a memory of when you felt this feeling.

I feel _____

Caleb's Feeling Emotions Example

When I feel _____ Angry _____	
What my BODY does	What I SAY
Kick	Swear words Call people names
How I LOOK	What CAUSED me to feel this way
	Feeling left out Thinking I am not in control
What I can do to CALM DOWN	How I WANT to LOOK and FEEL
Color, Read, Breathe Slowly	Happy

_____'s Feeling Emotions

Write your name here

When I feel _____

What my BODY does	What I SAY
How I LOOK	**What CAUSED me to feel this way**
What I can do to CALM DOWN	**How I WANT to LOOK and FEEL**

Caleb's Stay in Your Body Example

Sometimes when we have had sad or scary things happen to us, our bodies remember. Your body may remember by feeling as if you have left your body by going up and out of it. Other times, your body may not feel anything and it is as if your feelings have fallen down below your toes.

It is important to remember to stay in our bodies. We feel the best when we are in the middle of our bodies and aware of our whole body. This helps us stay in control of our feelings and behaviors by not going too far up or down in our bodies.

Example: When I feel scared or angry, I can feel myself floating up out of my body. When I feel sad, I can feel myself sinking down below my body. I want to feel in control of my body and stay in the middle near my heart.

_____'s Stay in Your Body

Write your name here

Instructions: Think of an emotion (example: angry, sad, scared). Do your feelings go up and out of your body or down and below your body when you feel this way? Choose a color and draw where your feelings go when you feel a certain emotion. Choose a different color and draw where you would like to be in your body when you feel this emotion.

Caleb's Thought Stopping Example

Thought stopping happens when *Negative Self-Talk* or thoughts are realized, stopped, and replaced with positive thoughts and healing self-talk.

I am not in Control

1. Draw or write: *Negative Self-Talk* (lie believed about self)

2. Color the stop sign as a reminder to stop the *Negative Self-Talk*

I can Control my thoughts and actions

3. Draw or write: Positive Thoughts or Healing Self-Talk (Truth)

4. Draw yourself believing and living the Truth

_____'s Thought Stopping

Thought stopping happens when *Negative Self-Talk* or thoughts are realized, stopped, and replaced with positive thoughts and healing self-talk.

	STOP
1. Draw or write: *Negative Self-Talk* (lie believed about self)	2. Color the stop sign as a reminder to stop the *Negative Self-Talk*
3. Draw or write: Positive Thoughts or Healing Self-Talk (Truth)	4. Draw yourself believing and living the Truth

Stress Scale

Instructions: Draw or write how you feel when you experience each emotion on the stress scale. (Example: Explosive—I feel out of control and want to break things.)

Think of ideas that will lower your stress level. (Example: Take deep breaths.) Use this scale to identify when you are stressed and ways to calm down when you are stressed.

5		**Explosive**
4		**Angry**
3		**Irritated**
2		**Bothered**
1		**Calm**

What Makes a Good Friend Checklist

Good friends…are respectful, responsible, and fun to be around. If you want to make or keep your friends, you must *be* a good friend:

- Good friends remember important things about their friends like birthdays and favorites
- Good friends do kind things for one another and use kind language
- Good friends help out when a friend is sad or has a problem
- Good friends like to spend time together
- Good friends have fun with one another
- Good friends take turns talking and choosing things to play
- Good friends remember the special things that their friends like
- Good friends do not put each other down or hurt each other's feelings
- Good friends can disagree without hurting each other
- Good friends allow friends to have other friends and talents

Draw yourself being a good friend.

Listening to My Body

How does each body part feel?

Check in with each part of the body to see how it feels right now.

Body Part	Example
1. Head	aches, dizzy
2. Mouth/Neck	tight, dry, hard to talk, lump in throat
3. Chest	fast breathing, hard to breath, tight
4. Heart	beating fast
5. Arms/Hands	shaky, making fists
6. Stomach	butterflies, aches, nausea
7. Hips/Butt	hard to sit, constipation
8. Legs/Feet	stomping, shaky, kicking

Choose a body part

What colors and shapes describe how this body part feels? What does it want to do? What emotion lives here?

Example: Hands are making fists.

- Color: red
- Shape: ball that is on fire
- Wants: to punch something
- Emotion: anger

Give a voice to the chosen body part

If this body part could talk, what would it say?

Example: The hands would say they need to fight to protect me.

What would make this body part feel better? What could be said to help this body part? (If possible and safe, do or say the things that would help the body part.)

Example: The hands would like to be rubbed. They would like to hear that they are safe and they do not need to fight.

Practice relaxing this body part

Example: Tense hands by squeezing tight into a fist for a few seconds, then release. Shake and wave hands for a few seconds, then stop.

Listening to My Body Worksheet

Choose a body part.	What are the colors and shapes of this body part?
What would this body part like to do?	What would this body part like to say?
What would make this body part feel better?	What I can do to help relax this body part?

What Are Your Negative Self-Talk Triggers?

Circle or color the *Triggers* that you have.

"I am not in control"

"There is something wrong with me"

"No one likes me"

"I am unlovable"

"My future is hopeless"

Negative Self Talk

"I am flawed"

"I am always bad"

"It is my fault"

"I will never be safe"

"God does not love me"

"If I were good enough, bad things would not happen to me"

Write additional *Negative Self-Talk Triggers.*

_____

_____

_____

What Are Your Triggers?

Circle or color the *Triggers* that you have.

Feeling scared, angry, or Vulnerable

Being alone   *Certain seasons*   **Birth of babies**

Men

Alcohol   Being touched

Certain smells   Shouting

Crowds

Loud noises   *Bedtime*

Nighttime

Broken toys

Being told what to do

Bathing

Adults   Specific holidays, anniversaries, or birthday

Parents leaving

Certain jokes, songs, or phrases   *Time of year when attachment break or trauma occurred*

Lack of routine   Family rituals or places associated with trauma

Write additional *Triggers*.

_____

_____

_____

Developmental Lost Experiences

Sometimes when traumatic, scary, or sad experiences happen in early childhood, children miss out on certain developmental life experiences. This is especially true when attachment has been disrupted. When thinking of common developmental experiences, a sense of loss may be felt. Children/teens that have developmental lost experiences often want an opportunity to re-do their childhood. It is never too late to have a happy childhood.

Developmental Experiences	Never Happened		Happened A Little		Happened A Lot		Wanted more of this	
Held as a baby								
Fed as a baby								
Played with as a baby								
Received gifts								
Celebration of birthdays								
One on one time with Mom								
One on one time with Dad								
Relationship with sibling								
Played with baby toys								
Played at the park								
Smiled at								
Had a home and bedroom								
Smelled pleasant things								
Felt safe								
Sang to and read to								
Had family pictures								
Baked cookies								

To determine a child/teen's lost developmental experiences, the child/teen (while thinking of their own experiences) can mark in the white space and the parent/caregiver (while thinking of the child's experiences) can mark in the shaded area for each developmental experience.

Use the checklist as a guideline for recreating positive developmental experiences to enhance the relationship between the child/teen and the current parent/caregiver.

Child/teen: _____ Date: _____

Parent/caregiver: _____ Date: _____

Creating Your Own Safe Place

Caleb invites you to create your very own *Safe Place*. A *Safe Place* is an imaginary place that you will make just for you. Some kids choose a forest, meadow, or even an ocean. Remember that you get to make all the decisions about your own *Safe Place*. Caleb's Safe Place is just an example. Once you decide where you want your *Safe Place* to be, you can create a home in your *Safe Place*. Caleb made a *Safe Tree House* to have in his *Safe Place*. In your *Safe Place*, you will make many things to help you heal from the sad and scary things that have happened to you. This is a place just for you and your *Hurt Self* (the younger parts of you that were hurt or confused).

In your *Safe Place*, you get to add a *Safe Tree House* or *Safe House*— whichever one you like the best. It can be a home within a tree called a *Safe Tree House*, a *Safe House* on the ground, or something else—you get to decide. When Caleb learns that he needs a place that is safe for healing, he loves creating his very own *Safe Place*. He hopes you also enjoy making your own *Safe Place*.

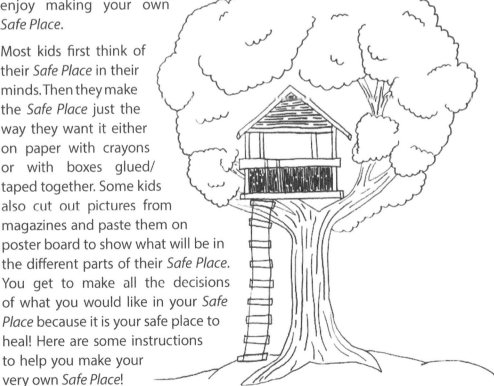

Most kids first think of their *Safe Place* in their minds. Then they make the *Safe Place* just the way they want it either on paper with crayons or with boxes glued/ taped together. Some kids also cut out pictures from magazines and paste them on poster board to show what will be in the different parts of their *Safe Place*. You get to make all the decisions of what you would like in your *Safe Place* because it is your safe place to heal! Here are some instructions to help you make your very own *Safe Place*!

Creating Your Own Safe Place Instructions

1. **Decide where to have your *Safe Place*.** You get to choose where you would like your *Safe Place* to be (meadow, forest, ocean, or another place). Caleb makes his *Safe Place* in a beautiful meadow that is calm and peaceful with flowers, trees, and sunshine. Caleb adds what he calls "Walls of Light" all around, under, and over his *Safe Place* so that no one could ever enter. The "Walls of Light" keep his *Safe Place* always bright and just the right temperature. Remember, you get to decide what you want for safety. Some kids have alarms, protective angels, and even special bodyguards.

2. **Design your *Safe Tree House/Safe House*.** Once you decide where to have your *Safe Place*, add your very own *Safe Tree House* or *Safe House*. After you choose if you want a *Safe Tree House* or a *Safe House*, you get to design the rooms inside the house just the way you want them. Caleb has six rooms in his house to help take care of his *Hurt Self* (the younger Caleb that was hurt or scared). His rooms include:

- Healing Room
- Kitchen with a bathroom off to the side
- Resting Room (like a bedroom but totally safe)
- Learning Room
- Nursery
- Fun and Games Room

Remember, you decide which rooms you want to have.

3. **Decorate the Rooms.** Now you get to decorate all the rooms in your *Safe Tree House/Safe House*. It is super fun to think of creative ways to decorate the rooms and what items to include in each room. For example, you can have baby toys in the nursery for your really little *Hurt Self*. Caleb adds all the toys he loves. He has bikes, video games, and more. You get to have everything the way you want it inside your *Safe Tree House/Safe House*!

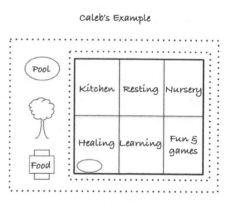

Caleb's Example

4. **Design the Outside.** Next, it is time to decorate the outside of the house and all the space that you have in your *Safe Place*. Caleb has an outside swimming pool, picnic tables with all different types of food and drinks, toys, games, and more. You can add different things or use what Caleb uses.

5. **Invite Special Helpers into the *Safe Place*.** Caleb also adds two special helpers named Brave Heart and Truthful Spirit—they are like angels. The special helpers in your *Safe Place* are super helpful because they cannot cause any harm, they know everything that happened to you, and they were created to help you. You can choose if you want to have Brave Heart and Truthful Spirit with you or other Special Helpers.

6. **Invite your Younger *Hurt Selves* to come.** Caleb receives help from Brave Heart and Truthful Spirit to bring his *Hurt Self* from the past into his current *Safe Place*. For example, when Caleb was four years old, he was really scared to be home alone. When Caleb makes his *Safe Place* in therapy, he imagines Brave Heart and Truthful Spirit going back to rescue his four-year-old self from the cold, dark room where he was alone. Then Brave Heart and Truthful Spirit take him to the *Safe Place*. Once Caleb's *Hurt Self* is in the *Safe Place*, the hurt four-year-old Caleb can heal and grow up safely. Now that you have created your very own *Safe Place* with special helpers, invite your *Hurt Self* to enter into a place of safety and healing.

7. **Use the *Safe Place*.** When sad or scary times happen, people tend to leave that part of them behind. Using the *Safe Place* is a way to bring all the parts of yourself back together. When you remember a sad or scary time from when you were younger, you can have your special helpers rescue you. For example, imagine Brave Heart and Truthful Spirit going back to that place in time where you were hurt. When they see your *Hurt Self*, they wrap you in a soft, warm light and bring you into your *Safe Place*. You do not have to go back in time because they will do it for you!

The first thing Caleb has his *Hurt Self* do in the *Safe Place* is to start in the Healing Room of his *Safe Tree House/Safe House*. Here, Caleb's *Hurt Self* heals the pain of being hurt. The Healing Room heals *Hurts* using a special healing water mixed with healing light and the hand of God. It is a good idea to heal right away when a *Hurt Self* comes into the *Safe Place*. After visiting the Healing Room, enjoy your new *Safe Place* as your *Hurt Self* learns, heals, and grows up to the age you are now! Some kids have more than one *Hurt Self*. You can invite all your *Hurt Selves* into the *Safe Place* for healing. Adults in your life might ask what your *Hurt Self* is doing in the *Safe Place* to celebrate how you are healing.

Congratulations! You have created a Safe Place for you to Heal!

Instructions for Creating a Grief Box

1. Gather supplies.
   - Box (we recommend a shoe box).
   - Paper.
   - Decorations (e.g. stickers, paint, glitter).
   - Writing tool (e.g. crayons, pencil).
2. Write Grief and/or Losses on the box.
3. Decorate the box.
4. Write or draw pictures of things you have lost due to *Early Hurts*.
   - Example: Lost experience—wanted to have a birthday party.
   - Example: Loss of important people—no longer able to see birth family.
5. Tell someone about your losses and feelings.
6. Give yourself time to remember your losses.

A Time to Remember: Grief and Losses

When thinking about grief and losses, it is important to remember a few things:

1. To heal from *Hurts* and the things we have lost, we need to talk about the losses and the feelings we have about the *Hurts*. Be sure to talk about your losses and feelings with trusted friends, adults, or a special helper.
2. Do not feel the losses and feelings all day long. Instead, spend only 15–20 minutes a day thinking about losses. Give yourself a scheduled time to think about the losses without letting it control your whole day.
3. Grief and losses can be worked on a little bit each day, and then the next day the feelings will still be there to work on some more. It is important to heal at our own pace to feel stronger.
4. Do not think about grief and losses right before bedtime because it can cause more bad memories to appear in your dreams.

My Grief Box

What would you put in your Grief Box? Write or draw what would be in your Grief Box.

Writing My Story

Complete the sentences about sad and scary things that happened to you. You can do this activity for each memory you have and as many times as you need. If you do not know some of the answers, that is okay. Remember, this is your story.

When I was younger some sad and scary things happened to me like when

_____

_____

Other hard things that happened to me were _____

_____

When the sad/scary thing happened, I thought_____

_____

I felt _____

I feared _____

I really needed _____

I really wanted _____

I told _____

I tried to tell_____

I remember _____ said _____

_____

I was confused about _____

I am still confused about _____

I am most sad about _____

I wish I would have told _____ that_____

_____

I wish I could tell_____that _____

_____

I wish that I could say _____

I wish that I would have said _____

If this ever happened again I would _____

These are the healthy things that I did to try to deal with the scary times

_____

_____

These are the unhealthy things that I did to try to deal with the scary times

_____

_____

Now I need _____

Now I want _____

I hope _____

One thing I learned from all this is_____

_____

Congratulations on writing your story!

Positive Things to Tell Yourself

I am a good kid

God loves me

Bad things can happen to anyone but I am not bad

I am going to work hard today

I am good at lots of things

Some things are harder to do than others, so I will try harder

I believe I can be whatever I want to be

I decide if I have a good or hard life

I am deserving of love and kindness

I am going to be kind today

I can be a great friend

It can be hard to live in any family, mine included

I will ask for help when I need it

I will not play games with my feelings or hurts

I will be kind and positive today

With God I can do great things

I can do this!

All kids have issues

All families have challenges

It is okay to feel grief and loss

Brokenness can be fixed

Changing Your Dreams

Tell a trusted adult about your scary or confusing dream. Then choose between these three options:

1. Draw a new ending for the dream that you would like better.

2. Draw something that you want to change in the dream from the time where the dream became scary or weird.

3. Draw a picture of what you wish you had dreamed.

Tell yourself during the day and at bedtime about your new dream and how you can Change Your Dreams! Complete these drawings as often as you need.

Draw your new dream here.

Common Challenges for Children and Teens Reassessed

	Symptoms	None		A Little		A Lot		All the Time	
1	Lying								
2	Stealing								
3	Food issues								
4	Anger								
5	Manipulation								
6	Troubles with friends								
7	Difficulty following rules								
8	Nighttime/sleep issues								
9	Grief/sadness								
10	Sensory issues								
11	Fear								
12	Safety								
13	Lack of trust								
14	Triggers								
15	Troubles with feelings								
16	Body aches/pains								

While thinking of a regular week, rate how often the common challenges occur. The child/teen can mark in the white space and the parent/caregiver can mark in the shaded area for each symptom.

> None – does not occur
> A Little – occurs 1–3 days of the week
> A Lot – occurs 4–6 days of the week
> All the Time – occurs every day, maybe even multiple times a day

Compare results to the common challenges previously identified. List improvements:

_____

Child/teen: _____ Date: _____

Parent/caregiver: _____ Date: _____

What Is in Your Heart Now?

Choose a color for each emotion. Color how your heart feels. You can also draw or write memories that are in your heart. When you have finished drawing What Is in Your Heart Now, compare it to your previous drawing of What Is in Your Heart.

Color the box that matches the emotion:

☐ Anger

☐ Fear

☐ Loneliness

☐ Happiness

☐ Sadness

HEALING AWARD

_____
Write your name here

is joining the Healing People of the World by Sharing his/her Healing Story.

_____
Write the date here

Congratulations!

$C\ a\ leb$
_____
Caleb

_____
Parent/caregiver

_____
Child/teen

HEALING ACTIVITIES AND ASSESSMENTS FOR PARENTS AND CAREGIVERS

Common Challenges for Parents or Caregivers

	Symptoms	None	Mild	Moderate	Severe
1	Difficulty communicating with child				
2	Personalizing child's behaviors				
3	Problems providing basic needs for child (food, clothing, shelter)				
4	Feeling frustrated or angry with child				
5	Feeling out of control				
6	Difficulty explaining attachment problems to family and friends				
7	Problems setting boundaries or rules with child				
8	Problems setting boundaries with adults				
9	Difficulty sleeping or fatigue				
10	Grief/sadness				
11	Marital/significant other troubles				
12	Fear				
13	Safety concerns about self or child				
14	Lack of support from others				
15	Triggers*				
16	Financial difficulties				
17	Troubles with feelings				

* See Trigger Checklist for Parents or Caregivers

While thinking of a regular week, rate the severity of the symptoms based on the frequency of the common challenges

> None – does not occur
> Mild – occurs 1–3 days of the week
> Moderate – occurs 4–6 days of the week
> Severe – occurs every day, maybe even multiple times a day

Scoring: Use the checklist to identify the top four challenges you have—starting with the most severe symptoms based on the level of occurrence. Use this as a guideline for working on your own healing.

Date: _____

Grounding Techniques

Parenting kids and teens with *Trauma*-related issues is hard work. Parents and caregivers often find themselves feeling *Dysregulated* (feeling out of sorts or out of control). When family members, including the one with attachment issues or trauma-related issues, are *Dysregulated* mistakes can be made. For example, saying and doing things that are hurtful or harmful to others. Here are some things you can do to regulate and feel more in control. When you stay regulated, you can continue doing this very important work of helping a child or teen heal from *Relational Injury*.

When you feel yourself becoming *Dysregulated*, it can be helpful to utilize *Grounding* techniques:

- Take deep breaths or blow out air
- Feel your feet on the ground or your body in a chair
- Focus on a certain point in the room
- Count to 10 slowly or count backwards from 10
- Hold rocks or sensory items
- Suck on a hard candy or chew gum
- Say a positive affirmation or prayer
- Call a friend to talk
- Go for a walk
- Take a bath
- Ask for help

Try a few that you have never done before. List your top four and commit to being grounded with your family:

1._____   3._____

2._____   4._____

Remember: Engaging in consistent *Self-care* might also assist in reducing times of *Dysregulation*. Some tips for *Self-care* include: get enough rest/ sleep, spend time alone, spend time with friends or a significant other, engage in healthy eating at regular times, and practice your faith.

Teach your child/teen these *Grounding* techniques also.

Coping Skills for Parents and Caregivers

1. First and foremost: Take care of yourself.
2. Guard your marriage and relationships with other children.
3. Learn as much as possible about attachment disorders.
4. Acknowledge and grieve your losses.
5. Ask for help.
6. Follow your gut.
7. Pick your battles.
8. Have "No Attachment Disorder" times.
9. Allow "down times" after therapy.
10. See the child behind the behaviors.
11. Keep a trauma/loss perspective: Don't take it all personally.
12. Create a safe home environment: Act with a plan, avoid sarcasm, squelch rage.
13. Make up for early lost experiences.
14. Say a helpful verse, prayer, or slogan during the day.

(Chara and Chara 2005)

The Five Rs

Realize attachment problems are rooted in *Trauma*-based feelings/thoughts and behaviors such as aggression, survival, or fear.

Reflection of *Trauma* feelings/thoughts is important.

Routines create safety.

Regular *Self-care* is necessary, especially for parents and caregivers.

Recognize *Dysregulation* and seek support.

Helpful Affirmations for Parents or Caregivers

This might be challenging but it is worth it

I am capable of parenting and loving this child

With God's help, our family can heal

God is in control

I can ask for help

Anything valuable is worth fighting for

This too shall pass

I have the resources to heal

I have the tools to help my child heal

We can get to the other side of this

That was just her trauma talking

That was just his hurt talking

I am a good parent

I can do this!

All kids have issues

All families have challenges

It is okay to feel grief and loss

Brokenness can be fixed

Triggers Checklist for Parents or Caregivers

It is common for parents/caregivers to feel strong emotions or to have *Negative Self-Talk* when parenting a child/teen with attachment problems.

Check the box for each scenario that causes you to experience *Negative Self-Talk* (negative phrases in your head that make you feel not good enough) or feel a strong emotion (e.g. sad, mad, fearful, incompetent). Complete the checklist about your own reactions to common events experienced when caring for a child/teen with attachment problems.

	Common Events for Parent/Caregiver Triggers	
1	Child misbehaves in public	
2	Interactions with own parents	
3	Memories of own childhood	
4	Kicking or hitting behaviors	
5	Yelling or screaming behaviors	
6	Stealing or lying behaviors	
7	Things are broken	
8	Lack of routine	
9	Arguing or manipulation	
10	Appropriate behavior by friends' children	
11	Being misunderstood or blamed for child's problems	
12	Child says "I hate you" or "I wish you were not my mom/dad"	
13	Fatigue	

After completing the checklist, identify your top four *Triggers* and explore situations in which these *Triggers* most commonly occur.

List your four top *Triggers*:

1._____ 3._____

2._____ 4._____

Common places *Triggers* occur:

_____

_____

We suggest that you have a plan prior to encountering these common *Triggers*. Ideas include:

- Complete relaxation skills
- Engage in *Grounding* techniques before and during times of *Triggers*
- Ask for another adult to accompany you to an event at which *Triggers* are likely to occur
- Other: _____

Family Bonding Activities

The purpose is to interact with your child while you are fully present:

1. Laugh over silly jokes

2. Blow bubbles together and try to catch them

3. Put lotion on each other's hands and feet

4. Trace each other's hands, feet, or body

5. Comb one another's hair or apply make-up

6. Hold hands and count to 20

7. Play musical instruments together and remain on the same beat (can also just tap on things to the same beat)

8. Pick two small toys or puppets and have the toys/puppets play together

9. Cook a snack together and eat the snack together

10. Complete a puzzle together (Choose a challenging but not too difficult puzzle to complete as a family. Then paste the completed puzzle together and put it on display in the home)

11. Say a prayer together

12. Complete an art project together

13. Play a favorite game together

14. Play children's rhyming games (e.g. Patty Cake, This Little Piggy)

15. Play Peek-A-Boo

Additional games you can play together:

Follow the Leader

Instructions: Take turns being the leader. Have the other person be the follower. Walk around with one person leading and the other following.

Mother May I/Captain May I

Instructions: Take turns being the mother/captain. The mother/captain stands at one end of the room with his/her back to the other participants. Participants take turn asking Mother/Captain may I _____ (example: take two giant steps forward, hop three times). The mother/captain either replies yes or no. If the mother/captain replies no, she/he can also say no but you may take _____(example: one baby step forward, two hops). Play until participant reaches mother/captain. Then switch roles.

Sensory Issues

It is important to distinguish problems that are rooted in a sensory processing issue versus *Trauma*.

Young children with sensory processing problems often are under-sensitive or over-sensitive to sensory stimuli. Some children seek sensory stimulation while others avoid sensory stimulation.

Check the boxes for sensory stimuli in which your child displays signs of over- or under-sensory sensitivity and also check the boxes for which your child either seeks or avoids sensory stimuli.

	Sensory Stimuli	Under-sensitive	Seeks stimuli	No concerns	Over-sensitive	Avoids stimuli
1	Strong smells					
2	Loud noises					
3	Tastes or food textures					
4	Light physical touch (gentle touch of face, clothing, hair)					
5	Pressure (hugging, firm grasp, wrestling)					
6	Hot temperatures (bathing, food, outdoors)					
7	Cold temperatures (bathing, outdoors)					
8	Pain (injuries exaggerated or ignored)					
9	Tickling					
10	Textures					
11	Sense of balance (loses balance)					
12	Body awareness (too high or low activity level)					

(Adapted from Chara and Chara 2005)

After completing this short checklist, if you notice multiple sensory concerns, we recommend seeing an occupational therapist for a further assessment.

Common Challenges for Parents or Caregivers Reassessed

	Symptoms	None	Mild	Moderate	Severe
1	Difficulty communicating with child				
2	Personalizing child's behaviors				
3	Problems providing basic needs for child (food, clothing, shelter)				
4	Feeling frustrated or angry with child				
5	Feeling out of control				
6	Difficulty explaining attachment problems to family and friends				
7	Problems setting boundaries or rules with child				
8	Problems setting boundaries with adults				
9	Difficulty sleeping or fatigue				
10	Grief/sadness				
11	Marital/significant other troubles				
12	Fear				
13	Safety concerns about self or child				
14	Lack of support from others				
15	Triggers*				
16	Financial difficulties				
17	Troubles with feelings				

* See Trigger Checklist for Parents or Caregivers

While thinking of a regular week, rate the severity of the symptoms based on the frequency of the common challenges

None – does not occur
Mild – occurs 1–3 days of the week
Moderate – occurs 4–6 days of the week
Severe – occurs every day, maybe even multiple times a day

Compare results to the common challenges previously identified. List improvements:

_____

Date: _____

Celebrate Healing

In the midst of working on healing from the pain and past hurts, it can be hard to think of the progress and positives along the healing journey. It is important to celebrate the small as well as big victories along the way. Take time to remember the progress your child has made and continue to dream of the healing that is to come. Celebrate your hard work and your child's hard work. You both deserve to be recognized!

Plan a celebration honoring your child's healing and your healing too. It does not have to be expensive or include a lot of people. You can invite as many or as few people as you want. All that matters is that you share in the joy of the healing that is in progress.

If this book has been completed in a therapy setting, you can celebrate the completion of the book by having a small party as part of the therapy session.

PART 3

RESOURCES

RESOURCES

Guidelines and Recommendations for Professionals

This book can be utilized in a variety of ways in a therapeutic setting.

GROUPS AND PEER GROUPS

Our professional experiences have shown us it is very beneficial for children and families working on attachment issues to meet with other children and families working towards the same goals of healing from *Relational Injury* and other *Traumas*. A group format is effective because children and teens heal as they learn they are not alone in their experiences. In addition, having another individual to share experiences with allows for healing from *Relational Injury* to take place through the development of trust and mutual support.

We recommend a peer group structure where children or teens (working on attachment and trauma) can meet together to read the book, complete activities/worksheets, and learn more about healing from attachment and trauma. In situations where participants are limited, we have found that even having a small group of only two members can be helpful.

We also strongly recommend that each group member also have family time as a part of therapy. This format could be adapted for in-home counseling, family therapy, support groups, school counseling, or at home with parents or foster parents.

MULTI-FAMILY GROUPS

A creative option for family healing is a multi-family group. This is when more than one family attends group therapy together. Often therapy and group experiences are helpful to all family members—even the siblings of the family member with attachment and trauma issues.

We recommend that the multi-family group format include times when a few families can meet together to read the book, complete activities/

assessments, and learn more about healing from attachment and trauma problems. Then, we suggest that the parents or caregivers spend time together while the children/teens work on activities together. This gives both the parents/caregivers and the children/teens time to share their experiences with others struggling with similar situations. If siblings are present, they can also meet together. This allows for entire families to engage with each other as well as individuals to connect with others in a supportive setting. At the end of each multi-family session, we encourage families to complete Family Bonding Activities (page 126) with their own family members.

WEEK-BY-WEEK GROUP FORMAT

The group format can be divided into several sections to promote healing. Each week during the multi-family group format, families meet all together in a large group for 20 minutes to read and discuss the chapters. Next, parents/caregivers and children/teens attend separate groups (siblings should be in their own group) for 40 minutes to complete activities and share their experiences with each other. Finally, individual families meet together at the end of the session for 30 minutes to complete Family Bonding Activities (page 126).

Week 1:

- Introductions and Goals of the group.

- Read Chapter 1.

- Both parents/caregivers and children/teens complete assessments (Start with Common Challenges for Children and Teens *and* Common Challenges for Parents or Caregivers).

- Begin Family Bonding Activities for each individual family.

Weeks 2–11:

- Read Chapters 2–7 at a group-friendly pace (some chapters tend to take more time) to address all the common challenges and complete related activities. It is important to tailor the sessions to fit the children/teens and families.

- Continue with Family Bonding Activities. We encourage families to complete a family bonding project over the course of a few weeks. For example, an art project or a puzzle that is challenging but not too difficult which can be glued together and displayed in the home.

Week 12:

- Review key concepts.

- Allow families to share their family story of healing and any completed family bonding projects.

- A party is also fitting for the last session. We suggest that food be brought by all families to share. The Healing Award (page 118) can also be given to the individual families and each family member.

Further Reading

Chapman, G. and Campbell, R. (1997) *The Five Love Languages of Children.* Chicago, IL: Northfield Publishing.

Chara, K. A. and Chara, P. J. (2004) *Amy Elizabeth Goes to Play Therapy: A Book to assist Psychotherapists in Helping Young Children Understand and Benefit from Play Therapy.* London, UK: Jessica Kingsley Publishers.

Chara, K. A. and Chara, P. J. (2004) *Sensory Smarts: A Book for Kids with ADHD or Autism Spectrum Disorders Struggling with Sensory Integration Problems.* London, UK: Jessica Kingsley Publishers.

Chara, K. A. and Chara, P. J. (2005) *A Safe Place for Caleb: An Interactive Book for Kids, Teens, and Adults with Issues of Attachment, Grief and Loss, or Early Trauma.* London, UK: Jessica Kingsley Publishers.

Forbes, H. T. (2008) *Beyond Consequences, Logic, and Control: A Love-Based Approach to Helping Attachment-Challenged Children with Severe Behaviors, Volume Two.* Boulder, CO: Beyond Consequences Institute, LLC.

Forbes, H. T. and Post, B. B. (2006) *Beyond Consequences, Logic, and Control: A Love-Based Approach to Helping Attachment-Challenged Children with Severe Behaviors.* Boulder, CO: Beyond Consequences Institute, LLC.

Levine, P. A. and Frederick, A. (1997) *Waking the Tiger: Healing Trauma.* Berkeley, CA: North Atlantic Books.

Levine, P. A. and Kline, M. (2008) *Trauma-Proofing Your Kids: A Parent's Guide for Instilling Confidence, Joy and Resilience.* Berkeley, CA: North Atlantic Books.

Siegel, D. J. and Bryson, T. P. (2011) *The Whole Brain Child: 12 Revolutionary Strategies to Nurture Your Child's Developing Mind.* New York, NY: Bantam Books.

Siegel, D. J. and Hartzell, M. (2003) *Parenting from the Inside Out: How a Deeper Self-Understanding Can Help You Raise Children Who Thrive.* New York, NY: Penguin Group.

Helpful Organizations, Websites, and Contacts

FOR PARENTS AND CAREGIVERS

ABC's of Child Development

www.pbs.org/wholechild/abc/index.html

Developmental milestones

ATTACh (Association for Training on Trauma and Attachment in Children)

www.attach.org

International coalition of professionals and families

Attachment Parenting Canada

www.attachmentparenting.ca

Canadian-based resource center for information about attachment parenting

Attachment Parenting International

www.attachmentparenting.org

Information and resources for attachment parenting support groups

Child and Adolescent Bipolar Foundation

www.bpkids.org

Help for families raising children with bipolar disorder-like issues

Compass Clinical Associates, PLLC

Urbandale, IA 50322, USA

contact@compassclinicalassociates.com

Tel: (515) 412-5112 (Bruce Buchanan)

Coram BAAF Adoption and Fostering Academy

http://corambaaf.org.uk

Information and resources for child placement issues in the UK

Evergreen Consultants in Human Behaviors/Attachment

www.attachmenttherapy.com

Therapy for attachment-disordered children

International Attachment Network UK
> www.ian-attachment.org.uk
> Attachment and human development information

Institute for Attachment and Child Development
> www.instituteforattachment.org
> Treatment, training, and child placement agency

LD Online
> www.ldonline.org
> Information and resources on learning disabilities for parents, teachers, and other professionals

Nurturing Parenting
> www.nurturingparenting.com/links.html
> Family development resources

Parents Active for Vision Education (P.A.V.E.)
> www.pavevision.org
> Information on vision problems, which frequently occur with sensory integration issues

Rape and Sexual Abuse Counseling UK
> www.rasac.org.uk
> Information and resources along with free and confidential support

Young Minds for Children's Mental Health
> www.youngminds.org.uk
> Resources, web links, and parent helpline

FOR PROFESSIONALS

Association for Play Therapy (United States of America)
> www.a4pt.org

Beyond Consequences Institute
> www.beyondconsequences.com

The Bowlby Centre
> http://thebowlbycentre.org.uk

British Association of Play Therapists
> www.bapt.info

Family Psychological Services P.C.
> www.playtherapy.ws

Play Therapy International

www.playtherapy.org/index.html

Play Therapy United Kingdom

www.playtherapy.org.uk

The Theraplay Institute

http://theraplay.org

Trauma Center At Justice Resource Institute

www.traumacenter.org

Glossary

Dysregulation: When a person feels out of sorts or out of control. Often the person feels overwhelmed by emotions.

Early Hurts: Sad or scary experiences that happened in early childhood. Also known as Early *Trauma*.

Grounding: Staying connected to the present moment and feeling appropriately regulated in your body.

Healing Behaviors: Behaviors that are appropriate, safe, truthful and good—for self and others.

Healing Beliefs: Beliefs that are true and good.

Healing Kid: Children and teens that work hard to heal from their past *Hurts*.

Healing Knowledge: The good and true things that are learned as one heals their *Hurt Self* and lives a life filled with *Healing Beliefs* and *Healing Behaviors*.

Hurting Behaviors: Actions, based on *Hurting Beliefs*, which cause harm to other people or yourself. Behaviors that keep people away, due to fear and mistrust, so that a person can feel safe.

Hurting Beliefs: Lies that a person believes because of past *Hurts*. False guesses that a person uses to try to understand the truth about past *Hurts*.

Hurts: The emotional or physical pain a person has after they have had sad or scary events happen to them.

Hurt Self: The "little child" inside a person who was hurt in early childhood. The part of a person that needs to be healed in order to overcome past *Hurts* and *Trauma*.

Negative Self-Talk: The negative and hurtful words or phrases that you tell yourself. They are often like a voice inside one's head saying you are not good enough.

Relational Injury: *Trauma* that either occurred in the context of a relationship or disrupted a relationship. Since *Trauma* disrupted a relationship, healing from *Relational Injury* requires a healthy relationship with another person as part of the healing process.

Safe Place: An imaginary place where a person, particularly that person's *Hurt Self*, can go to be healed.

Safe Tree House/Safe House: An imaginary house inside a *Safe Place*. A house where special helpers, such as Brave Heart and Truthful Spirit, can help a person heal from past *Hurts*.

Self-care: The daily act of taking care of oneself. Adequate *Self-care* allows a person to have more energy to give to their child during the healing process.

Trauma: An event or experience that had a negative impact on someone's life—a past *Hurt*.

Trigger: When a person is reminded of sad or scary experiences from his/her past. Sometimes a memory will flash before your eyes, your body will feel funny, or you will suddenly have a rush of emotions.

Some glossary definitions are adapted from Chara and Chara (2005).

Index

CPI Antony Rowe
Eastbourne, UK
May 18, 2021